A CAT ON A
BEACH BLANKET

THE INTRIGUING MYSTERIES OF LYDIA ADAMSON

Other books in the Alice Nestleton mystery series:
A CAT WITH A FIDDLE
A CAT OF A DIFFERENT COLOR
A CAT IN THE MANGER
A CAT IN THE WINGS
A CAT IN A GLASS HOUSE
A CAT ON THE CUTTING EDGE
A CAT IN A CHORUS LINE
A CAT IN WOLF'S CLOTHING
A CAT ON A WINNING STREAK
A CAT WITH NO REGRETS
A CAT IN FINE STYLE
A CAT BY ANY OTHER NAME
A CAT UNDER THE MISTLETOE

The Deirdre Quinn Nightingale mysteries:
DR. NIGHTINGALE COMES HOME
DR. NIGHTINGALE RIDES THE ELEPHANT
DR. NIGHTINGALE GOES TO THE DOGS
DR. NIGHTINGALE GOES THE DISTANCE
DR. NIGHTINGALE ENTERS THE BEAR CAVE
DR. NIGHTINGALE RIDES TO HOUNDS

. . . and the new Lucy Wayles mystery series:
BEWARE THE TUFTED DUCK
BEWARE THE BUTCHER BIRD

Lydia Adamson

A CAT ON A BEACH BLANKET

An Alice Nestleton Mystery

A DUTTON BOOK

DUTTON
Published by the Penguin Group
Penguin Books USA Inc., 375 Hudson Street, New York, New York 10014, U.S.A.
Penguin Books Ltd, 27 Wrights Lane, London W8 5TZ, England
Penguin Books Australia Ltd, Ringwood, Victoria, Australia
Penguin Books Canada Ltd, 10 Alcorn Avenue,
Toronto, Ontario, Canada M4V 3B2
Penguin Books (N.Z.) Ltd, 182–190 Wairau Road, Auckland 10, New Zealand

Penguin Books Ltd, Registered Offices: Harmondsworth, Middlesex, England

First published by Dutton, an imprint of Dutton Signet,
a division of Penguin Books USA Inc.
Distributed in Canada by McClelland & Stewart Inc.

First Printing, July, 1997
10 9 8 7 6 5 4 3 2 1

 REGISTERED TRADEMARK—MARCA REGISTRADA

LIBRARY OF CONGRESS CATALOGING-IN-PUBLICATION DATA:
Adamson, Lydia.
   A cat on a beach blanket: an Alice Nestleton mystery / Lydia Adamson.
      p.   cm.
   ISBN 0-525-94304-8
   1. Nestleton, Alice (Fictitious character)—Fiction.   2. Women detectives—United
States—Fiction.   3. Actresses—United States—Fiction.   4. Cats—Fiction.   I. Title.
PS3551.D3954C396   1997
813'.54—dc21   96–48596
                                                                                                    CIP

Printed in the United States of America
Set in Century Expanded
Designed by Eve L. Kirch

PUBLISHER'S NOTE

mystery

A CAT ON A
BEACH BLANKET

Chapter 1

ell, I made it through all the holidays. Just barely.

What I felt like doing on Thanksgiving Day was to join my old neighbor Mrs. Oshrin down at the community soup kitchen, where she volunteers her time. But I ended up at a big bash at my friend Nora's bistro near the theater district. Nora said it would be an unforgivable insult to her if I didn't show up. So I went and ate the lousy turkey.

I was a pretty cheerless soul on Christmas Day. But I had to do an acting job and join in the festivities at my niece Alison's brownstone. She and her companion, Felix, simply would not take no for an answer. So I went and sang the lousy carols with their skinny friends.

I rang in the New Year at a dull party with a man I had been seeing off and on for a year or so. I awoke the next morning with a champagne hangover and the resolve not to see him again.

It was a brand-new year, but Grandma Nestleton's little girl was not a happy little actress–cat sitter.

I had lost my bearings, so to speak. Nothing seemed to go right and nothing seemed to be right. I was tired of auditioning for parts I knew I wouldn't get. Tired of beating the bushes for cat-sitting jobs. Tired of social obligations. Tired of people. Even tired of my beloved loft.

But things have a way of changing—suddenly, almost like magic sometimes. And within sixty days of that grim beginning to the year, I was ensconced in a fantastic house on the beach.

A house worth millions, in the middle of what was referred to as the Gold Coast. All skylights and endless space and wood flown in from rain forests in the Pacific. Hot tubs and kilims and plush sofas and chichi modern art on the walls. And a mere fifty yards from the Atlantic Ocean, in Hollandia, a small dune community between Bridgehampton and Easthampton, on the South Shore of Long Island.

No, I didn't win the lottery.

A friend of a friend told me about this zillionaire stock trader named Littleton who, every year, hired a house sitter for his beach house during the months of March, April, and May.

It was a common arrangement in places like Hollandia. Storms, freezing temperatures, beach erosion, and vandals all made it dangerous to close the houses throughout the winter and into early spring. So the owners gave people who sought beach solitude—usually writers and painters—a rent-

free house for two or three months—until Memorial Day—
and a hundred and fifty dollars per month for expenses.

I packed up the cats and the biggest, fuzziest sweaters I
owned and I was out of Manhattan like a shot.

So I had a new trade. Alice Nestleton, house sitter.

The first two weeks there were wonderful. Just what I had
been craving: solitude. I took long walks on the frigid beach
and longer hikes to the general store that also functioned as
the post office. On sunny, windless days I even strolled into
the village, although most of the small, elegant stores were
still shuttered.

My cats were in heaven! What with all that glass, they
could bask or romp in the strong sunlight all day long.
Pancho, who usually chased or ran from imaginary enemies,
could focus instead on gull and geese silhouettes appearing
above the house. As for Bushy, my Maine coon, he was like a
pensioner in Florida—eating to his heart's content, sleeping
in any one of a hundred little nooks he had discovered, and
cuddling under the down comforter with me all through the
frosty nights.

And then, without warning, on the morning of March 21,
the novelty inexplicably vanished.

I awoke that morning, and instead of the powerful,
renewing sun, I saw nothing but dark clouds. It was bleak
and cold on that first day of spring.

I made coffee as usual, but it seemed to take me forever to
bundle up and get outside.

I climbed the wooden steps going up the high dune and
then down the other side onto the beach.

The tide was coming in, waves slamming the shore. The wind was blowing something fierce. The salty spray flavored my coffee. I could barely stand.

Edging away from the shoreline, I sought the shelter of the dune. And standing there, shivering, trying to inhale the warmth from a cup that had already gone cold, I suddenly felt pitifully alone.

I wanted out of all that solitude. I had had it with the romance of the deserted beach and the ocean. I had had it with introspection.

I wanted to be back in the crazy-quilt Manhattan struggle.

At the same moment that realization came to me, I stuck my free hand into my coat pocket. There was a crumpled piece of paper inside.

It was an invitation—actually, more a flyer than a personal invitation. Something I had received weeks before, my second day in Hollandia. But I had ignored it until then.

The paper announced a poetry reading at the Norris house—just west on the dunes. According to the invitation, there was a reading every Tuesday at 6:00 P.M., rain or shine or tidal wave. It was signed "Marla Norris."

People! Other human people! That's what the invitation signaled to me. It made little difference whether I was being asked to a poetry reading or a used-car auction. I decided to go.

I left my house at five-thirty that afternoon. There were two ways to get to the Norris house—by the beach or by the road. I chose the beach even though it was starting to get foggy and dark by then.

I climbed the dune and headed west along the shore.

Not more than a hundred yards from my house, a figure burst out of the fog, scaring me out of my wits.

But it was only a jogger; a woman I had seen running many times before, in fact. Behind her trotted a brace of Afghan hounds. She waved and was gone.

I walked on. Gradually I could make out the top of the Norris house, hidden, like mine, behind a massive dune.

Someone had placed a lantern by the wooden steps which went up and over the dune. A nice touch—helpful in the fog.

I had just started to climb the steps when I heard a bell—a faint, tinny chime.

I stopped.

The sound had come from the base of the dune, near the stairs.

It was a cat with a collar. The bell must have been attached to the collar. And what a homely cat it seemed in the dim light of the lantern.

She was long and yellowish, not young, with fierce green eyes. And she was feasting on a frozen, muddy, long-dead horseshoe crab.

Was she feral? Probably. Maybe a summer tenant whose owners had gone home without her.

"A good evening to you," I said.

Maybe not such a good evening for her, by the looks of things. Her belly was distended as if she was pregnant or had just delivered a litter.

"Will madame be having dessert tonight?" I asked teasingly.

This time she glared angrily at me, obviously in no mood for jokes—or company. So I continued my climb up the dune and over.

Marla Norris's dune house was different from the one I was staying in. Older, bigger—one of those many-storied structures with a multiplicity of balconies and turrets.

The wind cut into my back as I rang the bell.

Marla Norris opened the door immediately. She was a handsome woman in her late thirties, with a thick blue muffler wrapped many times around her neck. Her black hair was cut short and stylishly. I was not prepared for her explosive ebullience.

"My God, it *is* you! Alice Nestleton! What a wonderful thing! To have a famous actress right over the next dune!"

She grabbed my hand and shook it.

"I think you're exaggerating a bit. The 'famous' actresses are here in the summer. I'm just a humble house sitter."

"Don't be so damn modest. I saw you in something at the Brooklyn Academy of Music when I was living in the city. It was in 1984, I think. You were great!"

She paused and looked pained suddenly.

"But I forget the play," she added.

"So do I," I said.

Then she pulled me inside.

Chairs and sofas had been pushed into the center of the living room. A folding aluminum table had been opened and was laden with drinks and foods. There were four people in the room other than Marla Norris and myself—three women and a man.

They were all wearing outer garments as well as mufflers.

When I saw several of those portable plug-in radiators on the perimeter of the "circled wagons" I realized what had happened. Marla's heating system had gone on the blink.

My hostess pushed me into a big old red armchair, handed me a paper plate piled high with small sandwiches, and introduced me to the others as "the brilliant actress Alice Nestleton."

"This is Bea Verdi," Marla said, nodding at a beautiful wan-looking young woman in a green sweatshirt and hood. "Bea is a terrific poet," Marla added.

The lone man in the room—balding and burly—was Karl Drabek, who was, I learned, a painter.

Then there was Jenny Rule, obviously the oldest, who Marla said had written the world's greatest unpublished pasta cookbook.

And finally, there was Lillian Arkavy, a rather plain-looking woman with unruly red-gray hair. Marla laughingly described her as a full-time novelist and a part-time gossip. The name sounded familiar.

Marla then brought me a hot chocolate, to go along with the untouched sandwiches on my plate, and a snifter of brandy. My chair's tufted arms were getting crowded.

"So you're in the Littleton place?" Karl Drabek asked.

"Yes."

"I hate that man," Jenny Rule said.

"Who?" I asked, confused.

"Ivor Littleton."

"I never met him," I said. "We spoke on the phone a couple of times. He seemed perfectly nice."

"He's a mass murderer," she retorted.

"And a pervert," Karl said.

"And an extortionist," Marla chimed in.

"And a torturer of young tomato plants," Lillian Arkavy added.

"And a dynamiter who blows up church organs just to hear the noise," Bea contributed.

Then they all laughed crazily. It was obvious that the alcohol had been flowing for some time before I arrived.

Marla stood up, raised her hand, and said, "Enough. Let's get on with it."

Obviously, I had misconstrued the invitation. It was not a classical poetry reading; more a circle of friends sharing their latest efforts.

"Who'll go first?" Marla asked.

Lillian Arkavy sighed, finished her drink, put on a pair of glasses, and pulled a sheet of paper out of her purse.

I closed my eyes and listened.

It wasn't really a poem. More like a string of clashing images. Like sardines and roses. Bluebirds and rabid bats. Nails and sunsets. A haiku of contradictions.

When the poem ended no one said a word. Lillian took off her glasses and refolded the paper.

"Well?" she demanded.

"Incomprehensible but beautiful," Karl Drabek said. "As usual." Then he stood up. Obviously he had decided it was his turn.

A shiver went through me. What if they expected me to recite? That would be ridiculous. I had no poems in my bag.

Drabek announced, "Being a painter, I make no apologies."

"For what?" Marla queried.

"For what I am about to read," he said.

He took a group of index cards from his back pocket and began.

It was a very explicit erotic poem, quite lyrical. About a woman he had met and loved in Berlin in 1981. Her name was Annaliese.

The poem became more and more sensual. He spoke the words faster and faster and with increasing emotion.

And it ended with the bitter words that his memory of her had become hostile. "She was the candle in the Halloween pumpkin—blown out and cold wax."

Lillian applauded. Jenny Rule looked sad. Bea Verdi patted Drabek on the shoulder. Marla Norris stared morosely at one of the radiators. I nibbled a sandwich.

Then Bea Verdi stood up suddenly, as if it were futile to postpone the inevitable. She had one of those small wire spiral notebooks open.

First she gave an introduction to the poem: "As some of you know . . . or maybe none of you know . . . this is the second anniversary of Grumpy's death. He was a silly old black cat, but I loved him very much. A few nights ago I had a dream about him. That he was still alive. And out on the porch. I woke up and went outside. Of course he wasn't there. But I couldn't get back to sleep, so I wrote this poem."

She paused, looked at a place over our heads, then said, "I call it 'Just Grumpy.' It's very short."

She straightened her back, flicked off her hood, and began.

I scribbled your name upon the sand,
But the waves washed it away,
So I wrote it with a second hand,
This time the tide made it its prey,
"What a fool you are," I heard you say.
"Yes, Death does all the world subdue,
But our friendship shall live and later life renew."

There was a long silence.

"Sad," said Jenny Rule.

"Poor old Grumpy," said Karl Drabek.

I didn't know what to say. Bea Verdi had simply cannibalized a beautiful sixteenth-century sonnet by Edmund Spenser. It was one I knew well. I had had to learn it in a high school English class in Minnesota. The real poem started with "One day I wrote her name upon the Strand." The sonnet's name was "To His Love." Bea Verdi had paraphrased the first four and the last two lines, ignoring the middle eight, which are the pith of the poem.

"It was too short," noted Lillian Arkavy.

"Well, yes," replied Bea.

Then Marla Norris put her two cents in. "I didn't like it at all. It's not your regular style of writing, Bea. Your other poems I love. This was too old-fashioned, if you'll pardon the word. Mawkish. Yes, that's it. And too damn sentimental."

I have never seen a person of obvious intelligence and some sophistication react so badly to what was essentially mild criticism.

A mask of anger slid down over Bea Verdi's lovely face. And then a mask of rage.

She slipped the notebook shut, pulled her hood back on, and without another word strode out of the back door.

"Bea, wait!" Marla Norris called.

For some reason my heart went out to Bea Verdi.

Maybe it was because of her cat.

Maybe it was because I thought it strange but charming for her to have absconded with Edmund Spenser's sonnet without even mentioning the source.

Anyway, I went after her. I just wanted to tell her that her little ditty . . . her little poetical theft . . . was just fine with me. And I wished I could have met Grumpy.

Bea had left the back door open. I walked through and stood on the deck.

A fierce wind blew me halfway around. The sound of the waves behind the dune was alternately deafening and muted.

The back of the house was near the road, separated from it by a small square of concrete that functioned as a parking lot.

I could see her walking toward her car, fighting the wind at every step.

"Listen!" I shouted to her.

She stopped. Turned. Looked at me blankly.

"Your poem was very good! I really enjoyed it!" I yelled.

She gestured with her hands that she couldn't hear.

"Spenser, isn't it? Edmund Spenser!"

She shook her head. She couldn't hear.

"The poem! Your cat!" I yelled.

She made a gesture that it was futile. Then turned back, kept walking and opened her car door.

All I remember after that is the sudden flash of light and what sounded like thunder.

The blast blew me back into the house and into unconsciousness.

Chapter 2

The first thing I saw when I woke was a white wall. Then I saw a tall man in a blue overcoat standing by the window. It must be morning, I thought, because the sun was streaming through that window.

"You're in Southampton Hospital, and you're fine," the blue overcoat said.

I sat up. My eyes hurt. Then there was a kind of rolling ache along my forehead.

And then I remembered.

"The girl . . ." I whispered.

"She's dead, Miss Nestleton. You *are* Alice Nestleton, aren't you?"

"Who are you?"

"My name is Dayton Coop. I'm a homicide detective with the state troopers."

He had a long, mean face, and he spoke with a funny accent that I couldn't place.

"Are you sure she's dead?" I asked.

"Six army-surplus hand grenades were taped to the steering wheel of her car and then wired to the door handle. The pins were pulled the moment she pressed the release lock of the door. Yes. Bea Verdi is very dead."

A nurse came in, took my temperature, gave me some pills, and fluffed my pillow.

A volunteer came in, said good morning, and fastened a breakfast tray to the bed. Then she laughed.

Dayton Coop wandered over and inspected the breakfast. "It looks like they gave you a boiled egg," he noted.

I looked at the egg. Was a grenade shaped thusly? My eyes ached again. I could remember the horrid burst of color and flame.

"Dry toast," Detective Coop noted critically.

"What do you want?" I asked.

He took out a notebook and flipped the pages. He read off the names: "Marla Norris, Karl Drabek, Jenny Rule, Lillian Arkavy." He closed the book. "They all gave me statements. I just want to ask you a few questions."

"Ask."

"I want you to confirm what they said."

"Ask!"

"I mean, you were the last person to see Bea Verdi alive."

"Ask, damn you. You're making me weary."

I wanted to fling the boiled egg at him.

"Did anyone leave the house during this so-called poetry reading?"

"No."

"Did you hear anyone prowling around outside?"

"No. But there was a gusting wind."

"Did Bea Verdi talk about any threats to her person?"

"To me?"

"Yes."

"It was the first and last time I ever met her."

"Answer the question, Miss Nestleton."

"No, she never mentioned any threats to me."

"Tell me why you followed her out of the house. I mean, if you had never met her before, why go after her? What were you going to say to her?"

"She was angry and hurt. People had slammed her poem. I liked it, and I was going to tell her so. I just wanted to show support for her poetry."

"Are you sure that's the reason you followed her out of the house?"

"No, Detective. Now that you mention it, I was going to tell her the car was wired with hand grenades and I wanted to be there on the spot to see her blown to pieces."

He smiled. "I'll be in touch," he said.

After he was gone I stared down at the egg. I was hungry, true, but I had the strange feeling that if I took a spoon and cracked that egg open my breakfast tray and I would be blown to smithereens. I'd be no more than a shadow on the wall.

The nurse stuck her head in. "Your doctor will be here shortly. We'll get you out before lunch."

I leaned back in the bed. Poor Bushy and Pancho. They were waiting for their breakfast.

I closed my eyes and tried to sleep. The pain behind my eyelids was very soft and throbbing.

My grandmother, who raised me, used to tell me that my mother, who died when I was young, always said, "If there's trouble to get into, Alice will find it."

And that was when I was a toddler.

But a young poet blown to pieces upon opening her car door was a little more than just "trouble."

It was like all the chickens coming home to roost at one time.

Chapter 3

Bushy and Pancho were very angry at me when I came back to the beach house. Angry and hungry. They didn't want to hear any excuses or explanations.

I placated them with large blue-plate specials of tuna, chicken, and veal in gravy.

The sun was pouring through the house. The surf was muted. There was an overwhelming sense of spring coming and winter done.

I stood in front of a mirror on the north wall of the house. It was an "art" mirror, with curved borders.

What a mess I was! I didn't know whether to laugh or cry. A drama critic for a now defunct newspaper had once characterized me as "a long golden drink of water who fastens herself to a part like a leech."

Well, that was a while ago. I wasn't, according to the

current image in the mirror, a long golden drink of water anymore. Or rather I would say I was now a beaten-up gulp.

There were tiny bruises all over my face and neck from the explosion.

As for the very, very slight concussion, that wasn't visible at all except for some headache lines in my brow.

Suddenly, in the mirror I could see Bushy and Pancho watching me from their food dishes.

I turned around and chastised them. "You may not like what you see, but at least I'm in one piece."

Then I lay down on one of the plush sofas that dotted the interior of my beach "cottage."

The doorbell interrupted my daze about twenty minutes later.

It was Marla Norris, and when I opened the door she rushed right past me and began to pace in a kind of hysterical fashion, talking a mile a minute.

"We all wanted to come see you, Alice. But then we thought it might be too much for you. So I was selected. Is there anything I can do? It was so terrible . . . the whole thing is . . ."

And then she sat down suddenly and heavily on the same sofa I had just vacated.

"Would you like something to drink?" I offered, noticing that she was dressed in the same insufferably chic manner as the night before. As if the moment she got up in the morning a computer selected and delivered the top of the line to her. As if it were simply inconceivable that she would not be chic, no matter the circumstances.

"Do you understand how crazy this all is?" she demanded, apparently in response to my offer of a drink.

I nodded and sat down on the sofa beside her.

"I wish I could tell you what a wonderful young woman Bea was."

Bushy wandered over and leaped up, landing between Marla and myself.

"She came here about ten years ago," Marla continued, "from New York. She came here originally to do a story about this place—what it's like off-season. I mean, the nine months of the year when we don't have to deal with those idiotic celebrities who come here in the summer and pay the grocer with hundred-dollar bills for a bottle of skim milk. Bea came out here and fell in love with the place. And she stayed on here."

Bushy started to clean himself. One of his feet banged Marla. She banged him back. Shocked, he abandoned the sofa immediately.

Then Marla grabbed my arm tightly. "Do you understand what I'm saying? Bea Verdi was a wonderful person. She didn't hurt anyone. All she wanted to do was write her poems and publish them in those obscure little journals. I mean, who would murder a person like that? No one, right? You just don't kill sweet people like that. It . . . it isn't fair."

She released my arm then, and let out a manic laugh. "Here I am shouting and ranting—and I'm the one who was supposed to pay you a calming visit."

We sat for a long time in silence. The surf was picking up, like a low, rolling roar.

Marla finally broke the silence: "Did that detective speak to you?"

"Yes. At the hospital."

"What an idiot that man is," she said bitterly.

"Why so?"

"He didn't listen to me. I told him who did it."

That shocked me. "You mean you know?"

"Well . . . not really. I mean, it had to be a madman. So just check the state mental asylums. There's one ten miles north of here. Find who walked out. Find the mad bomber. That's what I told him to do, but I bet that moron didn't listen to a word I said. Don't trust long, lean men, Alice!"

She had a point. I once worked with a long, lean British actor in an off-Broadway play. He asked me to go to Brooks Brothers with him to select a jacket. He turned out to be a compulsive shoplifter of ties.

Marla stood up. "What must it feel like to be blown up like that? I can't imagine it. I can't imagine that beautiful young woman suffering so!"

"I imagine she died instantly," I said.

"No! You don't understand what I'm saying."

"I think I do!"

"Yes, of course you do. Please forgive me. I'm too upset to speak rationally."

Pancho whizzed past her.

"And it must be worse for you, Alice. You were right there! You saw it all."

"Yes, I saw it," I agreed. But in fact I had seen nothing but a sudden flash. I had *felt* it.

"A cup of coffee now would be good," she said.

"I'll make some."

She suddenly sat down again and her face became as white as a sheet.

"I keep thinking how terrible it was that I never taped those poetry get-togethers. We would have had Bea's voice with us. Because you know, Alice . . . oh, I'm sure you do know . . . if you have ever lost a loved one . . . the first memory that fades is what the voice sounded like. You remember how they looked and walked but not how they spoke."

I started to make the coffee. Bushy leaped back onto the sofa to redeem his Maine coon cat honor.

As I ground the beans I tried to remember Bea Verdi's last poem. But my brain was still addled.

Chapter 4

Nothing happened the next ten days. I rested and recuperated. The village seemed to have forgotten the bombing. No one visited me. No one questioned me. The weather grew inexorably milder.

For some reason, I never told anyone in Manhattan what had happened. I dropped the usual postcards to my friend Nora, my agent, my peripatetic lover Tony Basillio, and my niece Alison. But there wasn't even the slightest hint that poor old Alice Nestleton had almost become chopped meat. Why was I silent about it? To be honest, I haven't the slightest idea.

Why was the village of Hollandia silent? I think because the local villagers tend to treat all disasters like their ubiquitous hurricanes: When one hits, you bury the dead and forget about it, because another one is coming, and it'll probably be worse. Of course, when the beautiful people arrive, after

Memorial Day, the scenario changes. A stray dog gets side-swiped by a dune buggy and the village obsesses over it all summer long. Such is life at the shore.

Anyway, after ten days of recuperation, during which I thought of little except when the damn headaches were going to stop, my two cats mounted a vicious attack on me. On April 1, of all days—April Fools' Day.

The truth is that one or the other of them usually harasses me in the morning, pushing me to get up and feed them. But this morning they acted in concert, obviously having put aside personal differences in order to plan and execute the blitzkrieg.

First they started the customary prowling—back and forth near the bed. Back and forth. Throwing mean little glances at me.

I ignored them.

Then they both leaped onto the bed, not getting too close, mind you, either to me or each other. Then they began a concerted licking and chewing campaign on my sheets. Then they went into a staring and yawning campaign.

When that failed to rouse me, they pulled out all the stops. They scuttled off my bed, sharpened their claws loudly against the side of the sofa, and began the fake mouse hunt—trying to sound like a pride of lions.

When that failed they just stood next to the bed and began their operatic duet—cries, moans, gurgles, screeches, and sounds that go beyond the powers of human description.

I gave up. I climbed out of bed, went to the kitchen, opened their cans, and fed them.

Then I looked at the wall calendar. Yes, it definitely was April Fools' Day. I looked back in time. Yes, the bomber had struck just after the vernal equinox.

I looked forward in time. Easter was coming up. Then the Jewish Passover. Then daylight savings. Then Earth Day and Arbor Day.

In May there was May Day, when I usually dance around a pole. Then Mother's Day. And finally Memorial Day. The latter being getaway day for one Alice Nestleton, house sitter.

But getaway day was still a while away and the cat food was running out. It was time for the patient to wander out. I put on my floppy sweater and my floppier hat, grabbed a big canvas shopping bag, and headed for the general store.

The woman behind the counter, a kindly woman who limped badly, told me the cat food I wanted was depleted. Did I want the two cans left?

I didn't, and I headed toward town, feeling quite well in the breezy morning.

People in cars waved to me. I waved back. I hadn't the slightest idea who they were. It was just a custom in off-season Hollandia. People in cars waved to walkers—the latter being few and far between. It was as if the local motorists were honoring anyone eccentric enough to utilize foot power.

The main village of Hollandia was only three blocks long, anchored on the west by a gas station and on the east by an ancient little hotel. Between these anchors lay the stores, bars, churches, and small administrative buildings.

As I turned onto the main street just past the gas station, I heard some very strange noises . . . loud noises toward the center of town.

It was odd. The cars had also ceased. The main street was now empty of traffic.

The noise was clearly that of human voices.

Then my eyes focused. I pulled off my floppy hat. The noise was people talking and shouting. There was a crowd in front of the elegant white Congregational church in the center of town—the one with the high bell tower.

I walked closer until I had reached the outer circle of people.

Then I realized that this crowd was shouting at someone . . . who in turn was shouting back.

That someone was a young man perched high up and precariously on the top of the bell tower.

In the alley of the church a volunteer fire engine contingent was laying out a net and putting up ladders.

The young man kept threatening to jump. He seemed to be either totally drunk or totally deranged—or both. He alternately laughed, cried, or screamed between his threatening gestures.

Two policemen were on the roof of the church trying to talk the young man down.

There was a young woman standing alone by a disfigured elm tree. One hand rested on the tree, as if for support. Her eyes were fastened on the drama, but they were oddly blank.

"Who is up there?" I asked.

"Nick Frye," she answered.

The crowd gave a sudden collective moan as the young man made a threatening gesture—flinging himself out from the tower and then catching himself at the last minute. He was slender, with dark curly hair. His white T-shirt was discolored by sweat and dirt.

Then a police officer on the roof threw a pack of cigarettes up to the bell tower.

Nick Frye caught it.

"He wants to die," the young woman said in a monotone.

The latest threat to jump had quieted everyone.

"Do you know why?" I asked.

"Love," she replied bitterly. So bitterly that it frightened me a bit, and I stepped back.

But my curiosity overcame my fear.

"Love?" I queried.

She laughed a manic laugh, without moving a muscle.

"He loves a dead woman," she said. "He loves a woman who was blown to pieces."

My God! I realized she was talking about Bea Verdi.

I felt very strange, very disconnected. Was this whole thing an April Fools' joke? Or was it some kind of street theater? After all, Hollandia and the surrounding areas were always filled with theatrical people escaping from Manhattan.

Then the young man on the tower let loose a string of curses—at the onlookers, at Hollandia, at the world.

The crowd seemed to become hostile to him for the first time. One man taunted Nick, "Jump!" and then walked away. A kid threw a rock up at him.

I turned back to my informant . . . to ask her more questions. But she was putting on a pair of sunglasses in a manner that seemed to indicate our brief intimacy was over. Then she began to walk into the crowd.

Had she been telling the truth about the boy teetering high up above the world?

Why not? Why lie to a stranger? But it was odd that no one else had mentioned to me that Bea Verdi was involved with a young local. No one had said a word—not even the detective Dayton Coop.

The remaining crowd suddenly grew silent. Nick kept on yelling. The people below were no longer watching the jumper. They were watching a fireman stealthily climb up the far side of the tower.

Nick never saw him. But thirty seconds later he was in his powerful grasp, and the incident was over.

I went to buy my cat food—twenty-four cans. Then I started the long walk home.

About a mile from the dune house, I rested by the side of the road.

And right there and then, for the first time since that dreadful night, I remembered the cat in the dunes—the yellow cat with the distended belly, feasting on that dead horseshoe crab.

Oh my, I thought, I have to find her and her kittens.

The walk to the village, alas, had set back my recuperation a bit.

It took me another three days of convalescing before I could begin my cat-finding expedition.

I started out near Marla's dune house, because that was where I had seen Madame of the Bells, as I called her.

Then I slowly worked my way back toward my beach house, from dune to dune.

Once in a while I called out to the cat. Once in a while I whistled. All the while I kept my eyes open.

About two dunes from my house I decided to rest for a while and gaze at the ocean. I clambered over the lowest dune to the ocean side . . . and almost ran over three people seated on the sand staring out at the ocean.

They looked at me as if I were some sort of psychotic seagull.

"I'm really sorry. I had no idea anyone was here," I apologized.

My God! One of the people sitting there was that young man from the tower, Nick Frye. But now he was quite still. He sat with a very straight back—almost Zenlike. As if he were in meditation.

Next to him was a young woman with a broad kindly face and thick blond hair pulled back into a ponytail. She was wearing a leather vest.

Had I once worked with this young woman in the theater? I had a strong sense that I had met her before. If not backstage, then maybe at a party somewhere.

Suddenly I realized that she was the young woman in the village who had been leaning against the tree . . . watching the would-be suicide. No wonder she had been in shock. Nick Frye and she were friends.

Next to her was an old man smoking a crumbling hand-made cigarette. He wore brown coveralls and a bowler hat.

"I'm Alice Nestleton," I said. "I'm staying at a beach house near here."

The young woman said, "I'm Marge Towski."

I looked at her hard. She seemed not to remember me or recognize me at all. Or maybe she was playacting.

Then she pointed to the old man. "He's Harry Bulton." The old man nodded once at me, not speaking.

Then she pointed to the young man. "He's Nick Frye," the girl said.

Nick Frye didn't move an eyelash. They all continued their silent surveillance of the surf. It was as if I had barged into some kind of wake.

"I'm looking for a lost cat," I said. "A big old yellow cat with a bell around its neck. Has anybody spotted it?"

Marge Towski shook her head. So did the old man.

"Well, thank you anyway," I said. But I didn't leave.

I stepped back out of their line of sight and stared at the profile of the young would-be suicide.

Nick Frye was, I realized, a beautiful young man. It's not the kind of word that one uses for a man, usually. One says "handsome." But no, this young man was not merely handsome; he was truly beautiful. As if he were a potter's dream; one of those figures from classical Greek vases that suddenly had come to life. Yet one was perplexed by his beauty. Was he very vulnerable? He appeared to be. But at the same time his elegant frame gave off a sense of very strong resiliency . . . as if he could not be broken. He had a fierce beauty.

I wondered what he was thinking of now, staring at the ocean. Bea Verdi? His abortive suicide attempt? The forty-eight hours he must have spent in a psychiatric lockup?

Suddenly Nick and the young woman rose. From the way they moved I realized that they hadn't been sitting down on the sand; rather they had been squatting like Vietnamese.

They walked away without even a fare-thee-well.

"People around here," I said to the old man, "are either excessively friendly or excessively hostile."

Harry Bulton laughed and blew on the stub of his cigarette.

"You sit here often?" I asked him.

"Often enough. About every day for the last hundred years. I was sitting here when there was nothing but fishermen's shacks on the dunes. I was sitting here when the nets were dragged right down to the water during the striped bass runs. And I was sitting here when they banned commercial striped bass fishing because the damn fish got poisoned. And I was here when people like you bought the shacks and destroyed them and built those glass houses."

He really irritated me with that speech. "Get something straight, Mr. Bulton—or Bolton—or whatever your name is. I know you 'locals' don't like all the new people here with their money and their cars and their boats. But listen. I'm not one of them. And I'm not one of you. I'm just here as a house sitter, up to Memorial Day. Get it?"

The old man smiled, buried his stub in the sand, and started to roll a fresh cigarette.

I had the feeling I had gone too far in my response. "Look,

I'm sorry. I haven't been feeling good lately. I was standing near Bea Verdi when the grenades went off."

He arched his eyebrows at my explanation. He nodded sympathetically. He gestured that I should join him. I sat down and we didn't say another word to each other. We just stared at the surf.

This strange silence must have lasted a full ten minutes and two more hand-rolled cigarettes. I had no idea why I stayed there. My thoughts were on the young people who had left so quickly. There was something about this old man that intimidated me. I simply couldn't ask him to talk about Nick Frye and that Marge. I couldn't even ask him how the young man was faring.

He broke the silence with: "Don't get me wrong. I don't hate all those rich people in the dune houses. It's just that they're peculiar. They don't think like us working people."

Well, at least I was now being perceived as one of the "working" people.

"I never see you at my station," he said.

"What station is that?"

"My gas station."

"I don't have a car," I replied. "You mean you own that station at the edge of town?"

"No. Not that one. The one about a block north of Main Street, near the railroad."

I had seen it. A small two-pump gas station that I wouldn't patronize if I did have a car.

"And Nick works for me. Changes oil, pumps gas three or

four times a week. And Marge puts a few days in. At the stand."

"What stand?"

"Just off to the side of the station. Farm produce. Berries in season. You like berries?"

"Sure."

He rolled another cigarette. He put it in his mouth but didn't light it. He waved a hand toward the surf.

"Packed like blueberries in a box," he said.

"What?"

"We were talkin' about berries. And it reminded me of the runs."

Dimly I perceived he was back to his fish story.

"You know how tight they pack berries in a box? Well, the stripers were packed closer in their runs."

He was becoming excited. His hands started poking at the air.

"Sometimes I would be on the beach at night and the run would start. And the stripers would move fast along the shore. And the water was lit by the full moon. And you could see them just beneath the surface—all silver and powerful."

He stood up suddenly, the memory of the stripers exciting him, and his two hands tried to mimic the ripples of the fish so that I would understand. It was as if he were dancing for me. But then he realized he could not truly show me the way it used to be. He lit his cigarette finally, then doffed his hat to me in an excessively old-fashioned gentlemanly way and ambled off.

* * *

It was that same day, hours later, about ten o'clock in the evening, when I heard the frantic knocking on the door.

I was watching a cable movie on Littleton's enormous TV set when the knocking began. I didn't answer the door for a while. Not because I was frightened, but simply because the knocking was so rhythmic I thought it was some kind of bird or animal thumping on the roof.

When I did open it, I saw the young woman I had met so briefly on the dunes—Marge Towski.

"I need your help, miss," she said. Her voice was an inch from hysteria.

"What's the matter?"

"It's Nick! He's drunk again. He has a gun. He says he's going to kill Karl Drabek. He says Drabek murdered Bea."

"Then call the police!"

"No. I can't do that. They'll lock him up. Please! Please help."

"What can I do?"

"You know Karl Drabek. Come with me. Tell Nick he's no murderer, that he's a kind, good man. Tell him anything."

"You have something wrong. I don't know Karl Drabek. I met him just once."

Marge Towski gave me one of those cosmic looks . . . a look that said if I didn't help her now the trees would not bud. She seesawed a kerchief over her head as I made up my mind. Did I really have a choice?

She drove very fast. I kept talking to her to try to get her to slow down. But it was futile until I asked, "How long had they been lovers?"

"Who?" she barked back.

"Bea and Nick."

"Who told you that crap?"

"You."

"That's not what I said! They weren't lovers. Oh, Nick loved her. That's for sure. He spent twenty-four hours a day mooning after her. But she just played with him . . . strung him along . . . treated him like a silly kid. No, they were not lovers."

We pulled up in front of a small wood-frame house in the marshy land between the ocean and the bay.

The front yard of the house seemed to be littered with derelict car hulks.

But there was something about them that made me pause and stare.

"He's a fine artist," Marge said.

Yes. Now it was evident to me. They were a kind of sculpture. The fenders splayed to make the dead vehicles look like live, fearsome birds. My! They were quite something.

I followed Marge inside. It looked like a derelict house. There were only a few pieces of old furniture, and the shades on the windows were filled with holes.

Nick Frye was seated at the kitchen table, cleaning a handgun. He didn't greet us. He was wearing a gray sweat-shirt and dungarees, but no shoes or socks. His curly hair was wet, as if he had just showered. There was a drunken smile on his beautiful face. For the first time I noticed that his eyes were blue.

Marge walked close to him. She started to put a hand on

his back, then thought better of it and pulled her hand away. "Listen, Nick. This is the woman we met in the dunes today. She knows Karl. She knows he didn't kill Bea."

The stuporous grin never left his face. In a minute he began to whistle.

Marge gestured to me. I stumbled. What the hell was the script?

Ah, yes, that Drabek was innocent.

I slid onto the kitchen chair across from the young man. "Nick, listen to me. Karl is a friend of mine. He would never do such a thing."

Nick turned to me. He didn't really look or smell drunk. Crazy, maybe.

"Who the hell are you?" he asked, peering through the barrel of his weapon.

"I'm Alice Nestleton. I live in a dune house right by Karl Drabek's. Believe me, he's no killer."

"Oh, he's a killer all right," Nick said. His voice was oddly childish. "He wired those grenades to the door and blew Bea up. He did it! I know he did it. He did it because he couldn't have her, because she loathed him."

I looked quickly at Marge. She shrugged. We both knew that the young man should be getting some serious help. Ten days after his fantasy lover is murdered he decides to kill himself. He fails. Three days after that the vision of the murderer comes to him and he decides on vengeance.

Nick reassembled the weapon, pointed it at the ceiling, and pulled the trigger. The gun was not loaded.

Then he rammed a clip in. He worked the bolt. The gun was now loaded. He laid it reverentially on the table.

"You know what I would like, Marge? Some chocolate. It's in the refrigerator."

Marge nodded. But she didn't move.

"And I would like to see Bea once more. Just once more, Marge. Do you understand?"

Nick then gave out a kind of pathetic strangled cry and jumped up from the table. He picked up the gun.

"Wait," I said desperately. "I'm telling you, Karl Drabek isn't the killer. If he was, why would he have offered a fifty-thousand-dollar reward to find the killer? It doesn't make sense. It can't be a ruse. No one suspects Karl except you."

It was a bald-faced lie. But it worked. Nick's resolve began to unravel. He started mumbling, and in a few minutes he was crying helplessly, piteously.

Marge handed him a piece of chocolate. "Alice will find the killer," she said to him fervently. "Believe me, Nick. She was almost blown up herself. And she knows those people. They're her kind. Just be patient, Nick. She'll find Bea's murderer." She looked over at me. "Won't you?"

I didn't answer. Nick was now staring down at the loaded gun on the table. The tears were rolling down his cheeks.

I had an almost overpowering desire to push Marge aside and put my arms around the young man. It should be me comforting him, I kept thinking. Me brushing away his tears. Me.

But all I did was watch.

Chapter 5

So there I was the next morning, trudging over the dune to visit Lillian Arkavy. The purpose of my visit? Simple. The commencement of my investigation into the murder of Bea Verdi.

But who was fooling whom?

Sure, I had been hurt, physically, by the murderous bombing. But the "instructions" to conduct the investigation were not given to me by a homicide detective, or even by a friend of Bea Verdi.

No, they had come from a desperate young woman who was willing to promise anything to keep a friend from doing something self-destructive.

Would I have followed instructions if Marge Towski had told Nick that I was going to sail the Atlantic from Hollandia in a reinforced cornflakes box?

Besides, they weren't really instructions. They were a

plea. I walked along the crest of the dunes. Maybe, I thought, it all has to do with that silly old cat with the bell, whom I couldn't find again, and who might have been a figment of my imagination.

As my old friend from the NYPD, Rothwax, would have said: "If you think like a Cat Woman you're going to end up hallucinating like one."

Lillian Arkavy's beach house loomed up in front of me. I had selected her as the first port of call because I remembered how Marla had introduced her to me as a full-time novelist and part-time gossip.

Yes, I needed a good gossip now.

She was on the porch doing some kind of weird pseudo-martial-arts exercise. A tight sweatband bunched up her red-gray hair.

I stood still and watched. She wasn't very graceful. Not at all like . . . I was startled by what had popped into my head. I was about to compare her with Nick Frye in his elegant suicide dance on the bell tower.

What is the matter with you, Alice Nestleton? Why was I thinking of that young man? Was he the reason I was standing in front of Lillian's dune house now?

She saw me. She waved me up vigorously, without breaking the continuity of her exercise.

I climbed the redwood stairs and sat on a chaise. The morning was beautiful. The breeze was soft. The surf was quiet. When she had finished she unscrewed an elaborate ceramic thermos and poured us two cups of delicious tea.

"I'm so glad to see you again," she said. "I sent flowers to the hospital, but you had been released by the time they arrived."

Then she looked me over critically.

"Well, you don't seem to be really scarred," she announced.

"They're healing fine," I said.

We sat and sipped the tea in silence. It was quite pleasant.

"Marla," she finally said, "tells me you are quite an actress."

I gave her my standard response: "I am considered one of the finest perpetually unemployed actresses in New York."

It usually made people laugh. Lillian, however, didn't find it very funny. She grimaced. So I changed the subject to her. "You know, your name is familiar to me. But I just can't remember the titles of your novels."

She smiled. "The novel was *In a Meadow*. It was published about fifteen years ago. Then there was a book of short stories called *Bright Brown Eggs*. Both were about being young, female, American, and promiscuous in Paris and Rome. Both were critical successes and severe financial debacles."

She raised her cup in a toast to them and continued, "Then about ten years ago I published a crime novel about a widow who goes to live in rural Georgia and becomes involved in dismemberment, matricide, and a few other joys. It got made into a television movie. I made a bundle. I came out here. I bought this house. I act like a wise old lady novelist. I write poetry. I watch the tides. I wait."

She refilled our cups.

It was time for me to get to the point. Bluntly.

"Someone told me that Karl Drabek was in love with Bea Verdi."

"That's about the stupidest thing I ever heard in my life."

"You mean it's not even a remote possibility?" I persisted.

"It's about as likely as a whale walking out of the ocean during the next ten minutes and asking us if we have any whale food in a can."

"And the same person who told me that thinks Karl Drabek murdered Bea because he was crazy in love with her and decided that if he couldn't have her, nobody else would."

"That's even more ridiculous."

"Is it? Why?"

"Look. I know Karl Drabek. The man's a successful painter—which means he's a hustler. Painters don't fall in love anymore. They have other fish to fry. Believe me, Karl is incapable of what you call romantic love. And it would have to be the most extreme kind of such love to end in murder. Wouldn't you agree?"

I didn't reply.

"Let me explain something to you, Alice. You must understand. There's going to be all kinds of wild speculation about who did it, because if it wasn't one of us who killed Bea, they'll never find the murderer."

"Who do you mean by 'us'?"

"I mean all of us in Marla's house that night."

"None of us could have booby-trapped the car," I said. "Obviously Bea's car was okay when she arrived. And once she did arrive, nobody left the house."

"Exactly. So someone walked up to Bea's car while we

were all inside, wired it, and walked away. What about fingerprints? The blast wiped them away. What about car tracks or
footprints? The dune winds cover all such tracks in five minutes. You see, it seemed like such a primitive murder. But it
really was quite sophisticated. It was very much the perfect
murder. Maybe there wasn't even a motive. Marla believes it
was a psychiatric patient."

"By the way, did Karl and Bea ever date?"

"No. Not to my knowledge, anyway. They were not
really—how shall I say this?—compatible. Not intellectually,
at least. She didn't like his paintings and he hated her
poems."

She flung the remains of her tea out over the deck onto
the sand.

"Would you like some breakfast, Alice?"

"No thank you. I have to leave. Just one more question."

"Shoot."

"Have you ever run across a stray cat in the dunes? Yellowish. Maybe pregnant. With a bell around her neck."

"Now let me see. I've run across spiders, poisonous
grasses, crabs, gulls' nests, fornicating summer people, a
snake or two, and ant nests. But a cat with a bell and a belly-
ful of kittens? No."

I was standing, ten minutes later, directly behind Marla
Norris's house.

In fact, I was standing on the exact spot where Bea Verdi
had opened the car door and blown herself up.

The problem was—there was nothing left. The space was pristine.

When I looked up, Marla was staring down at me like a mother hen on an errant chick.

"Don't stand there like that," she warned. "Come up!"

I noticed that her house had been rearranged, all the portable radiators disposed of, and all the windows and doors flung open.

"I'm spring cleaning with a focused vengeance," she announced. "Sit there!" She pointed to the counter stool near the walk-through kitchen. Marla was wearing a stunning spring cleaning ensemble—all yellowish and flowery.

"I am about to grind an incredible new coffee bean," she said, beginning to measure the beans out.

"I was just at Lillian Arkavy's," I said.

"How is she doing?"

"Fine. She was very helpful."

"Helpful? Lillian? Are you sure? Lillian is smart. She's funny. But I've never known her to be helpful. Well, you live and learn. Besides, this is the seashore. Anything can happen—right?"

"Marla, do you know a young local boy named Nick Frye?"

She stopped measuring the coffee beans. She looked at me strangely. "Why are you asking about him?"

"Just curious. I had wandered into town the day he decided to jump off the church tower."

"Well, all I know about Nick Frye is that he used to do chores for Bea and he followed her around like a puppy— when she let him. He lives in that sinkhole between the bay and the ocean. A lot of the old fishing people moved there after they sold their land. I've never been out there but I heard the houses sink three inches a year. And his place is sinking fastest of all, because he makes crazy sculptures and lets them sit in his yard."

"Why do you call him a puppy?"

"Because that's what he looked like. You know—tongue hanging out and all."

"Marla, I'm going to ask you what might appear to be a very strange question."

She burst out laughing. "Oh, you actresses are all the same . . . the world over. On the one hand you often use a kind of excessive formality. 'I am going to ask what may seem a very strange question,' you say; all very prim and coy. And then you want to know exactly how many times I slept with the guy. And why. From formality to intimacy with nothing in between. Do they teach you that in acting school?"

"I wasn't aware I always do that." How, I asked myself, could Marla possibly know what I *always* do? We barely knew each other.

"Go ahead. Ask your question. I assume you asked it of Lillian also."

"Do you think there is any possibility whatsoever that Karl Drabek murdered Bea?"

"No. Never."

"Did it ever occur to you that Karl was in love with her?"

"Never."

"Why not?"

"Because the world is round, not flat. Because two and two does equal four. Because—"

"All right, Marla. I get the point."

"Does Lillian agree with me?"

"Yes. She thinks Karl is incapable of romantic love."

"Only an old novelist would use that phrase in polite conversation."

"What phrase?" I inquired.

"Romantic love."

Then she went back to her exotic coffee beans. But only for a moment. She pushed them aside and sat down next to me.

"I don't know what the hell you're doing, Alice Nestleton . . . wandering around the dunes asking stupid questions about a chubby middle-aged painter. As if he were some sort of dark prince of the dunes."

"I like that phrase, Marla. Dark prince of the dunes. We can bring an English actor in to play him."

Marla raised one finger to her mouth to caution me against something.

"But I will tell you one thing about Karl Drabek that I have never told anyone before. Deep down . . . way deep . . . he is one of the most lecherous men I have ever met. So, Alice, it is entirely possible that in some way he was pursuing that lovely young woman. Do you understand me? I mean, that is what lechers do. They pursue. They always pursue. And they never give up."

"Nor do they kill," I noted. "Lechery is indiscriminate. There's always another body to fix on."

"How well you put it!" Marla said.

"I have always loved the way the word 'lechery' sounds," I said.

"You *do* need a cup of coffee. Or the dunes will get to you and you'll spend your last few house-sitting weeks in Hollandia wandering from beach house to beach house looking for answers to questions you can't even formulate."

She burst out laughing again at her own words.

"Actually, now that it's spring, I feel more kindly to all the lechers of the animal world. And they are legion, my dear Alice."

All I could say was "Amen."

It was noon when I reached Jenny Rule's small squat beach house. Like many of the newer ones it was startlingly plain, relieved only by a single slanted skylight in the roof.

She didn't seem surprised to see me. Nor did she seem happy. Jenny was older than I had thought her, maybe sixty-five, and that day she was wearing a dowdy robe and Tibetan sandals.

She looked like she had just gotten up or had never gone to sleep.

The house was furnished minimally. The moment I walked inside my eyes darted to the kitchen, looking for the huge pots. I have always had an affection for huge pots. And after all, hadn't Marla Norris said that Jenny had written the world's greatest unpublished pasta cookbook?

Anyway, there wasn't a pasta pot in sight.

Jenny had her lovely gray hair done in a bun. Her figure

was still shapely and slender though there was that touch of an arthritic cast in the arms and shoulders.

"Sit down," she said. "I was just about to have some apple-cranberry juice."

I sat down on a high-back rattan chair. A small tapestry rug was under it. Jenny brought two mugs of juice. She handed me one and sat across from me in the matching chair.

The juice was terrible. About twenty minutes away from going bad.

We sat in silence. When I realized she wasn't going to say a word, I asked: "Do you walk on the beach often?" It was just meant to get the conversation going.

She seemed to be evaluating my question as if it were important or relevant to something. She stared glumly at her mug of juice and then rotated it slowly in her hands.

I realized then I had walked in on a very serious depression. I didn't know what to do.

She shifted uncomfortably in the chair. Then she said, "Ever since Bea died I have been having the strangest dream."

Her voice had that telltale affectless tone.

"In the dream I am standing on a street in Waltham, Massachusetts. That's where I was raised. It is not winter but suddenly the snow starts falling.

"The street and the people and the cars are all soiled and used. Dirty, blemished. But the snowflakes are ravishingly white, and soft, and lovely.

"The flakes fall all around me but none of them land *on* me. Do you understand?"

She stared into her mug before continuing.

"As I am standing there amidst all this soft, almost inde-scribable beauty, it suddenly dawns on me that each flake is all that is left of a dead person. Maybe the soul. Maybe the spirit. Maybe some undefinable substance.

"And then I wake up in a cold sweat."

I didn't say a word.

"What do you think it means, Alice?"

"I don't know."

"Is it some kind of vision?"

"I don't know."

"That poor girl. I suppose when they start killing the poets, the world is really doomed, isn't it?"

She closed her eyes and began to sway slightly in her chair, mourning Bea Verdi.

I had to get out of there or I was going to catch her virus. But I didn't know how to extricate myself.

So I changed the subject on a whim . . . to lighten the proceedings.

"Tell me, did you ever see a funny-looking feral cat in the dunes, with a kind of off-yellow coat and a bell around its neck?"

She sat up so suddenly that I mimicked the move.

For a second, only a brief second, I saw a shadow of fear breaking through her depression. And then she just closed her eyes.

"Did I say something wrong? I'm sorry."

"Oh no," she replied, waving one hand feebly. "It's just that what you asked reminded me of that poem Bea recited.

About the cat she loved. That's all. No, I never saw a feral cat in the dunes. Never saw a cat with a bell."

I left then, without ever asking even one pertinent question.

I was weary of the dunes and the beach, so I took the road home, walking along the edge where the grasses were shooting up in their spring vigor. There was a delicious smell in the air.

I was halfway to my house when I heard a car behind me. I moved even farther off the road to let it pass.

But the car never accelerated. It remained behind me. I turned and looked at the vehicle. The moment I did turn, the car stopped and a tall lean man stepped out.

It was Detective Dayton Coop. He made no move to approach me, nor I him. We were about twenty feet apart.

"Going for a stroll, Miss Nestleton?" he asked. He wasn't as old as I'd thought he was when he questioned me in the hospital room. But his face was lined from sun and wind. More like a sailor than a homicide detective.

I didn't reply immediately, because there was something about the tone of his voice that rankled me.

Finally I said, "Actually a slow jog."

He unwrapped a piece of gum. "I hear you're making all kinds of new friends around here," he said.

"I'm a sociable person."

"Yeah. I see a lot of actresses out here once the season starts. You people sure *are* sociable."

He put the gum into his mouth, grinned maliciously, and

added, "Sometimes you people are so sociable it just takes the breath away."

"I'm in a hurry," I said.

"Can I give you a lift?"

"No, thank you."

"Anytime you need one, just ask. After all, one has to be nice to the prime suspect."

"Are you serious? Me? The prime suspect?"

"Just making a little joke."

"It's not funny."

"Of course you *could* have wired that car, Miss Nestleton. After all, you were the last one to arrive at the beach house that night. You could have simply booby-trapped the vehicle and then just walked right in. In fact, that might be the reason you followed Bea Verdi outside. Because you wanted to see the carnage. You wanted to see the fruits of your labor."

Then he got into his car and drove past me. Soon the vehicle was out of sight.

His absurd speculation unnerved me. I left the road and climbed one of the dunes to stare at the surf. I soon realized that I was only about a hundred yards away from Karl Drabek's beach house. It was nestled between two dunes like an ugly gray turtle.

"Why not?" I said out loud. "Why not?"

I strode across the dune and banged on the door. He had no deck.

Drabek answered the door in a sweatshirt with torn-off

sleeves, sandals, and paint-streaked black chino pants. He looked balder and burlier than the last time I had seen him.

Yes, he had that little lecherous smirk at the corner of the mouth as if stating that all women who visited him, no matter the reason given, were there really for only one thing.

"Come on in," he said happily. His unshaven face was thick and handsome. His forearms were very muscular given his age.

The house was divided in half by function. One side was the studio, an incredible mélange of canvases, paints, rags. The other half was an equally messy living area with a table, small bed, huge overstuffed sofa that had seen better days, and file cabinets instead of chests. Oddly enough, the small kitchen was a model of orderliness.

He led me by the hand around the loft as if on inspection, then pointed me to the sofa. I sat down.

"Are you fully recovered?" he asked.

"I suppose so."

"I would imagine your head felt like Quasimodo's bells."

"Only a bit more melodic," I noted.

"What do you think of my hovel?"

"I like it," I said, which was not really a lie.

He launched immediately into a monologue about his old loft on Stanton Street in lower Manhattan.

Then he pulled out two of his newest paintings and showed them to me, as if he were exhibiting prize heifers.

They were huge and quite impressive. He painted in what I imagined was the hyperrealist school with just a dash of surreal elements. These two were the insides of Manhattan buildings—their lobbies and the various occupants of the lobbies.

He pushed these two paintings out of the way and started searching for another one.

I called out to him as he was searching: "Do you know Nick Frye's work?"

He waved a hand contemptuously. "Juvenile! Not even primitive. But then again, I think old cars should be shredded."

I leaned back and closed my eyes for a spell. When I opened them Karl Drabek was staring at me.

"I don't think you came here to see my work."

"No, I didn't."

"In fact, I have suddenly the overwhelming intuition that you're not here on a neighborly social call, either."

I didn't answer.

"You know," he said bitterly, "we painters have, above all, very developed intuitions."

He strode to one of the file cabinets, calling out in an ugly voice, "I'm going to give you what you want! Look!"

He opened the cabinet and pulled out two small ugly round objects.

"Is this what you're looking for? Huh? Have you been listening to the gossip?"

"What gossip?"

"You know damn well that I blew that poor girl to kingdom come because she wouldn't crawl into my bed. Here! Look!"

He came close to me and shoved the objects under my nose.

"What are these?"

"Bombs, my dear," he said in a mock-melodramatic voice.

Then he burst into laughter and dropped them onto the sofa beside me. I cringed.

"Don't be a fool. They don't go off unless you light them. They're fireworks. I use them to scare the gulls away. That's how the rumors started that I'm an explosives expert. And that's why some idiot is spreading the story about me and Bea."

I relaxed a bit.

"Let me explain something to you, Alice. Hollandia is a wonderful place for me. It has sand and surf and sun and seasons. There's only one trouble with it. A population of vicious rumor mongers."

He picked up the two fireworks and took them back to the cabinet, slamming them shut inside.

He turned back to me, smiling.

"By the way, if you really want to know who killed Bea Verdi, I'll tell you. Some deranged local who never forgave us for putting up houses where their fishing shacks used to be. Of course, no one ever forced the idiot to sell the land, and he probably made a bundle. But now he drinks all day and he nurses this hatred and one day he just snaps and wires grenades to the car of the loveliest person in Hollandia. I'll bet the idiot didn't even know whose car it was."

He brushed imaginary dust off his hands.

"So, Miss New York Actress, why don't you just get out of here and come back again when you want to read a poem."

I walked out of the beach house, feeling stupid.

But at least I knew what to do next: assure Nick Frye that Karl Drabek had no part in the gruesome murder of Bea Verdi.

I literally ran back to my house and called one of the town cabs.

Then I stood by the door and waited for the sound of the vehicle approaching.

What was my rush? Why was I so anxious to put myself in harm's way? That beautiful young man was violent and unpredictable. Oh, there was no question about that.

So why? I didn't know.

Chapter 6

The young man was coiling a rope in the front yard when my cab pulled up.

Nick didn't open the cab door for me. He didn't even come to greet me. He just stood there fiddling with the rope.

I waited for a moment at the ramshackle gate. Had Marla really called this young man a puppy? It hardly fit. Nothing really fit.

For the first time I noticed that the grotesque sculptures in his yard were painted, not rusted. And humans were represented as well as birds. What a difference in styles and studios between Nick and Karl! I wondered if Nick chose to work with derelict auto heaps or was forced to because they were the only material he had access to. Then a very bizarre thought popped into my head. What if the murder of Bea Verdi was not about love or hate? What if it was something totally different? Something to do with the natural world?

Something cosmic? Whoa, Alice, I thought. You are going around the bend. You are getting dune sickness—too much sun.

We were only five feet apart—separated by the gate. A wind started to blow. I found myself mesmerized by the movement of his hands. I looked away, toward the dismal house. There were fifteen or twenty equally dismal little houses in the enclave. It felt like being on a very poor Indian reservation.

"Where's Marge Towski?" I asked.

"I don't know," he replied.

"What are you doing with that rope?"

He gave me a self-deprecating little smile. "I'm going to hang myself." Then he looked at me slyly, as if to evaluate my response. All I could think was that he was no longer a boy and not yet a man, and that was what was so wonderfully strange about him. He *was* the cliché and it was quite beautiful. And poisonous.

Then suddenly he dropped the rope. He was finished with it. He folded his arms and stared at me—a bit defiantly.

"Where's your gun?" I asked.

"Hidden."

"You're too violent," I said, and then realized it was an amazingly stupid comment. My language with this young man seemed retarded. I found it difficult to speak to him. But I wanted to. I also wanted to touch him—to ease the raw wound of hurt which was so visible. The young man almost throbbed with the psychic pain. He was like a standing sore of grief.

"I have bad news for you, Nick."

"Is there any other kind of news?"

"Your theory doesn't hold water."

"What theory?"

"Karl Drabek didn't kill Bea."

"So you say."

"And he wasn't in love with her and they really had nothing to do with each other."

"I know what happened."

"You know nothing, Nick. Believe me."

"Why should I believe you?"

"Because I talked to people who knew them both. I tried to confirm what you said . . . what you believed. There was no confirmation at all. There was no romantic involvement. There was nothing of what you say."

"Marge listens to you. I don't listen to you, lady. I don't know who the hell you are. I don't know why Marge asked for your help. Maybe Marge needs help. I don't!"

"He didn't kill her, Nick."

"Then who did?"

"I don't know. Why don't you let the police worry about that?"

"The police? You know, I think you're a very stupid woman."

Why didn't I just walk away? Why was I taking this young man's verbal abuse? He was talking as if I had promised to find the killer and reneged on that promise. His memory was bad. But then again, he had other things on his festering mind.

"You're just like Bea's friends. All those poor fancy ladies eating their fat-free muffins. God, I hate them!"

His attack went on and on. I listened and took it as it became more personal and even scabrous. And I took it. Odder still, I felt no anger.

When he finished his tirade against fate, womankind, Hollandia, and a few other topics, he just walked into the house, slammed the rickety door shut behind him, and left me standing there.

The errant child spurns the protective mother. Was that what this was all about? Alice Nestleton had found a surrogate son.

I didn't know what to do. Should I go through the gate, pick up the coil of rope, knock on the door, and try to reason with him? About what?

Or should I get into a cab and go back? What cab? I had to call one. Where was a phone? Inside Nick's house.

Worse, there was the sad fact that my certainty of Karl Drabek's innocence in Bea's death was not what you would call a rigorous certainty. It was all smoke—a conclusion based on people talking to people.

I started to walk home. It was a very long walk and I was a bit unsure of my way. But I knew the general direction and I knew where the sun sank toward afternoon.

The land was flat. There were still a few working farms. The road borders were beginning to green and flower.

I walked, swinging my arms, trying to get that Nick out of my head. He was, as my grandmother used to say, like a slap in the face: It hurts but you get over it fast.

Well, maybe. But I had already fulfilled my slap quota—what with the grenades and all that. Lord knows I had the scars to prove it.

It was late afternoon when I saw the dunes in the distance. What a long day it had been.

I could pick out the roofs of the beach houses now. Mine was easy to spot; it was so charmingly ugly.

Even though I was weary, I approached from the beach side. I always tried to approach from that angle, as if I were a mermaid of mythological proportions, stepping out of the ocean.

Twenty yards away I knew something was wrong. Very wrong.

The doors were wide open. All the doors.

I ran into the house. Everything inside was crazy—thrown about . . . flung . . . broken.

"Bushy! Pancho!" Where were the cats?

Then I saw goofy gray Pancho seated on the kitchen counter gazing philosophically out over the carnage.

But Bushy—my Bushy—was gone.

I ran out of the house screaming his name like a madwoman.

It is hard to remember it exactly as it happened. There was no question that I "lost it," as the saying goes.

After I ran out, I just started to circle the dwelling, looking for Bushy and calling his name again and again.

Then I walked back into the trashed house and started to interrogate Pancho. "Where is he? Who took him? Why didn't you protect him?"

Pancho didn't say a word. He just maintained his gaze. That really got me mad. After all, this Pancho usually spent his entire day hysterically sprinting away from imaginary enemies. And then, when a real enemy turns up, he just curls up and becomes a philosopher—a Buddhist philosopher.

I had to compose myself. I had to think. Maybe Bushy hadn't been kidnapped. Maybe the wrecker just left the door open and the cat had wandered out onto the dunes.

It was growing dark. The house was beginning to stink, because the person who had committed all this carnage had not forgotten the kitchen and the refrigerator. There were milk and meat and eggs and fruit dumped all over the floor.

The sofa had been slashed and upended. I wondered what the owner would say when he saw it. Something had been smeared onto the walls in a circling pattern. I didn't know what substance it was—and I didn't want to know.

"Now Pancho, I want you to stay right where you are and keep your eyes and ears open. I'm going out to find Bushy. *Do you hear me?*"

Why did I keep talking to Panch? I don't know.

Then I recovered two unopened cans of cat food and marched out onto the dunes, banging the two cans together to attract Bushy, wherever he was.

What a strange sight I must have been to the gulls and the seabirds. A tall blond woman banging cat food cans unmusically. And a stranger to boot.

Between melodic riffs I called his name. At least this time I knew I was looking for a real live cat—my own Bushy—not a mysterious cat with a bell, whom I might have constructed out of my imagination.

As I searched, my reason and acuity returned. I understood what had happened: I had been warned. The beach house had been trashed as a warning and a threat.

I was being told not to ask any more questions about the murder.

Nothing infuriates me as much as coercion. It is the only thing that makes me brave.

On I trudged. Up and down the dunes. Banging my cans together.

Which one of them had done it? Karl Drabek? Jenny Rule? Marla Norris? Lillian Arkavy?

I had questioned them all. Any one of them could be the trasher. And the trasher no doubt was also the murderer.

It was strange how every single one of them had a theory and in their theories the bomber was always someone "out there." A vengeful drunken local. A release from the neighboring asylum. Not us, they seemed to be saying. You can't possibly suspect any of us.

As the night wore on these speculations ceased, because as each hour passed without my recovering my Maine coon there was a greater chance that he had in fact been catnapped.

I grew exhausted and crazed. Each step became torture. The cat-can symphony became erratic, mournful.

Finally—it was sometime past midnight—I could not proceed anymore. I simply climbed to the top of a dune and collapsed, facing the ocean.

When I opened my eyes again, I saw a wondrous thing. At the shoreline was Bushy the Magnificent.

He was crouched and playing with the incoming and outgoing tide.

He was so engrossed in his sport that he didn't see the madwoman hurtling toward him until he was safely imprisoned in her arms.

I carried him home and did not release my grip until he was safely in the house.

Then I just stood for the longest time in the center of all that debris.

War had been declared on me, I knew. There were two options. Run or fight. It was past the negotiating stage.

I chose to fight. But I was so very tired. And not a little frightened.

What about the police? Should I call them and report the break-in? They would consider it a robbery, ask me for a list of missing valuables. But I knew nothing was missing.

This break-in was about terror. And this terrorist wasn't a buffoon who would leave fingerprints all over. This was someone who had meticulously and brilliantly booby-trapped Bea Verdi's car.

No! No police. My head started to droop.

"Fatigue and fear doth send a good woman to bed—any bed." Who said that? I didn't know. But how true it was!

Chapter 7

slowly restored the beach house to its pretrashing state. I
stayed inside and rested. Once or twice a day I took a slow
walk to the surf.

No one visited me. No one phoned. It was as if the world
had dropped away. Was that really a bad thing?

Well, on the one hand it was quite salutary. After all, I was
weak and frightened by the break-in. So it was a chance to
regroup and buttress my resolve to find a killer.

But the isolation did reinforce my loneliness . . . my sense
of being alone in the world. Which was not true. Not true at
all. I think this lovely place, Hollandia, does it to you. The
dunes and the surf are isolating. The landscape seems to act
like a compass on the emotions. Everything points to one's
aloneness. Oh, it is very hard to explain. You see, the feeling
is not *really* loneliness . . . it is desolation, that bus-station-at-
two-in-the-morning kind of desolation.

Oh, I am beginning to babble like the archetypal out-of-work actress in a coffeehouse. But this was no Greenwich Village cappuccino joint; it was a million-dollar dune house in Hollandia.

Anyway, it was on the morning of May 1 that I commenced my formal, focused investigation into the murder of one Bea Verdi, the wounding of one Alice Nestleton, and the subsequent threat through house trashing against the same Alice Nestleton.

I felt healed. I felt rested. In fact, I felt downright joyous.

And it was May Day.

I picked up Bushy and Pancho and we danced around an imaginary pole in the living room.

Not too many people know that cats love to dance. They particularly like—how shall I say—earthy, almost pagan dances. That morning we danced to the beauty of spring and to the strangely compelling young man called Nick and to the sad dune cat with the bell.

And yes, we danced to the success of the Cat Woman (as I was known to the NYPD).

Then I proceeded to implement the first rational step in the investigation: find a local friend, namely Marge Towski.

I left the house and walked to the part of the dunes where I had first come upon the trio—Nick Frye, Harry Bulton, and Marge.

Two-thirds of the trio were there—Marge and the old man. Nick was not to be seen. The two greeted me warmly. We chatted. The old man reminisced once again.

"You don't seem to spend much time at your gas station," I remarked to him.

He laughed. "That's what I hired Nick for." It was obvious that Harry Bulton was not enamored of his current occupation.

"How's the farm stand doing?" I asked Marge.

"The first good melons have come in," she replied.

"Is someone watching the stand when you're out here?"

"Not now. Until the summer people get here, we're only open early morning and late afternoon. Just a few hours a day."

I invited them to lunch. The old man declined. He said he had places to go, errands to run. Marge hesitated at first, but then agreed.

We sat there for another half hour in the delightful spring breeze. There were many joggers and walkers along the shore.

"Another few weeks," the old man said bitterly, "and all the summer people will be here."

Then he sighed and added, "Well, I suppose they have to live too. God bless them!"

Marge and I walked back to my place. Once inside and seated, she appeared uncomfortable. It was a perceived class thing, I realized. Marge knew I was just a house sitter, but after all, I had been hired by one of "them."

"You have two options, young lady," I announced. "Tuna salad on seven-grain bread. Or tuna salad on seven-grain toast."

"Toast," said Marge.

I started to prepare the food, keeping the conversation going. "How is Nick? Calming down?"

"He seems fine. But it's probably just the calm before the next storm," Marge noted.

"Does anyone look after that young man?"

"No, he looks after himself. That's why he's so damn skinny. His mother lives with a new boyfriend on the North Shore. His father went up to New England after the striped bass fishery collapsed here. He was lost at sea, cod fishing."

"I'm sure you try and look after him," I said.

"I do. But no one can look after a fool."

"Amen," I agreed.

Then I served the sandwiches. We both sat on the sofa, the coffee table between us.

Bushy watched us, hoping for a chance at the tuna. "He's a beautiful cat," Marge said.

"Yes, he is. And he knows it."

She waved her hand as a gray blur of Pancho went by.

"What's his story?"

"Dementia," I replied. "A simple case of total dementia."

We finished eating. I served coffee and a piece of store-bought rhubarb pie.

I asked, "Why did Bea Verdi seem to be so isolated out here?"

Marge shrugged as if she found the question incomprehensible.

"I mean," I explained, "other than Nick following her around, she didn't seem to have any friends."

"That's not true. There was the Norris woman."

I sat up straight. This was something new. Marla Norris had not mentioned a special friendship with Bea. Nor had the others. "You mean Marla Norris—my neighbor?"

"Yeah. Oh, she and Bea used to be great pals. Bea used to get all her hand-me-down designer dresses. When you saw them from a distance you couldn't be sure who was who."

"And then did something go wrong?"

"I don't know. They just stopped being friends."

"It happens."

"With Bea I imagine it happened a lot."

"Why do you say that, Marge?"

She started to reply and then stopped, as if she were about to transgress. Then she said it anyway. "That lady was a fake. Don't you understand?"

"You mean Bea?"

"Yes. Nick used to talk about her night and day—about how smart she was, about her poetry, about all the journals that published her work, about all the awards she'd won. It made me sick. So one day I decided to check up on her. I don't really know why I did it. Anyway, I went to the library and looked in a few of the indexes of the literary journals Nick had mentioned. She wasn't there. She wasn't there with even one poem. I looked through every kind of poetry index you can imagine, and I didn't find one listing of one poem by a Bea Verdi. The woman was a phony."

"Did you tell these things to Nick?"

She shook her head, and before I could say another word, she just ran out of the house.

I sat and stared at the small piece of rhubarb pie she had

left on her plate. I was stunned. The sudden flood of new facts
was much more than I had expected from Marge Towski. I
had to think.

It wasn't the tuna fish that kept me awake that night. I had
digested it well. And I had also digested without difficulty my
new information.

That Marla Norris had never disclosed she had once been
a close friend of Bea Verdi's didn't mean much on the face
of it. There could be many reasons for her not to disclose
that fact.

And as for Bea Verdi's having dramatically inflated her
reputation as a poet—well, that kind of thing was common
enough. Particularly in places like Hollandia, where many of
the millionaires are in some kind of art or entertainment
business. They seem to go to great lengths to appear to be
serious artists whom the world just chose to throw money at.

No, what kept me awake that night was Nick Frye and the
dune cat with the bell. I kept worrying about both of them. It
wasn't in the manner I worry about my cats. Something different. I had the feeling that I knew something about them
that I had to impart to someone in order for them not to
suffer. Yes, it was a very strange, convoluted feeling.

At midnight I got up and walked outside. The night was
still and dark. The surf was muted; a slow, low lapping sound.

I walked away from the house and sat down on the crest of
the nearest dune.

Why wasn't I thinking of Tony Basillio? Why wasn't I
missing him?

The clouds parted a bit and the moon peeked out. A Minnesota moon, I thought, and then was astonished at the thought. What does a Minnesota moon mean? Home. A home long gone.

The moon vanished again. A breeze came up. I stood and started back toward the house.

Suddenly I heard the strangest sound in the distance. I stopped and listened to it. But it was gone.

Another two steps and the sound came again, carried on the breeze.

It was the soft tinkling of a bell.

Was it the feral cat? The mother cat hunting for her lost kittens?

I felt a surge of joy. I turned around and walked quickly over the dunes toward the sound.

The sound of the bell waxed and waned. I kept moving toward it, stopping when it stopped, moving when it started up again.

The night was becoming cool. The surf was beginning to pound. Sweat was now on my forehead and there was a chill in my body.

Then it vanished completely. I kept turning in place, my ears straining.

Another sound came on the breeze. It wasn't a bell this time but the sound of boots crunching on the packed sand.

I became frightened. I started toward the house. The footsteps became louder and closer. I walked faster and then broke into a run.

But I had lost my bearings. I kept climbing over one dune after another, but I didn't find the house.

Then the footsteps vanished. I calmed down. I tried to situate myself geographically, using the sound of the surf as a compass point. I projected the correct path and started on it.

I hadn't gone fifty feet along a dune when my right foot banged against some debris and became entangled in it.

I yanked my foot free just as the moon peeked out again. I looked down.

It was a funny kind of debris. A human body sprawled out on the sand.

It was Jenny Rule. She was dead, her eyes wide open, her forehead crushed by bullets.

She wore only a long pink nightgown with a bow on the bosom. Her bare feet were beautifully shaped.

I knelt down beside her. In the hollow of the neck someone had left a tiny bell.

I began to rock.

The message, I knew, was for me. It said in tinkling tones that the next corpse in Hollandia would be Alice Nestleton.

The elegant digital clock read 3:10 A.M.

For the past three hours my dune house had been the center of the investigation. Technicians and police officers trekked from the dunes to my house and back again—using my phone, using my bathroom.

Now it was emptying out. The floor of the house was littered and filthy, but the corpse, out there on the sand, no doubt had been removed fastidiously.

By three-thirty the only one in my house other than Bushy and Pancho was Detective Dayton Coop. He was walking about the inside of the house, peering into things and smoking furiously, one cigarette after another, snuffing them out in inappropriate places.

Finally I said to him wearily, "If you want to search the house, why don't you just say so? In fact, why don't you get a search warrant? And if you want to smoke, why don't you go outside?"

He stubbed out his latest cigarette on a saucer, then walked to the door, opened it, flung the butt out onto the dunes, and closed the door.

"You're getting to be quite a problem, Miss Nestleton."

"Me? No, I'm not the problem."

"Sure you are. Sure you are. Every time you take a breath of night air someone seems to get blown up or shot to death. Don't you find that strange?"

I didn't respond. Bushy was now in my lap and glaring at the tall detective.

"So let's run through it again. I know it's late. But actresses always keep weird hours, don't they?" He laughed at his own comment before continuing, "Take it from the top."

"I couldn't sleep. I went out for some air."

"And this was about midnight?"

"Approximately."

"And then . . ."

"Then I heard a bell."

"A bell. Church bell? Dinner bell? Sleigh bell? Loud? Soft? What?"

"A small tinkling bell. And I remembered that feral cat I saw in the dunes the night of the Verdi murder. She had a bell too. So I thought it was her and that she needed help or food. I went toward the sound."

He pointed to the seat next to me on the sofa. "Do you mind if I sit?"

"Not at all," I said, but I moved one cushion away and Bushy made a little sound that was more snarl than meow.

Coop settled into the fabric with ostentatious sighs, as though if he hadn't sat immediately he would have collapsed. But that was, I knew, his pathetic attempt to get me off guard. There was no question about it—this man didn't like me and didn't trust me.

"So there you were," he said, "standing on the dunes in the beautiful night, and you hear the bell and you go in pursuit of it. Sounds mythological, doesn't it? Like the siren who lured men to their death with beautiful music."

"It was just a bell," I said harshly. "It was the cat I wanted to find—I wasn't following any beautiful music."

"And did you find the cat?"

"No. Not the cat or the tinkling bell, Detective."

"So then you started walking home."

"Yes. Except I wasn't walking. I was running."

"Why run?"

"Because I heard footsteps behind me. Someone was out there. I was frightened."

"Why should you be frightened, Miss Nestleton? You've

been staying out here for some time now. What did you have to fear?"

"My house was broken into awhile ago, trashed completely. It was a warning to me. So I've been on edge."

"A warning," he mused. "Really? Did you report that to the police?"

"No."

"Are you sure it wasn't just a robbery?"

"Nothing was taken."

"Maybe the thieves were frightened off."

"I'm telling you what the break-in was about, Detective. You believe what you want."

"I'll be finished here shortly, Miss Nestleton. I know it's been a long day. Just be patient. Now, where were we? Oh, yes . . . so you heard the footsteps and you ran back to the house."

"That's what I said." I watched him play with another cigarette, rolling it around in his fingers. But he didn't light it.

Pancho knocked over the newspaper stand, but no one paid him much mind. Detective Coop replaced the cigarette in his pack and took out a stick of gum.

"And then," he said, "you stumbled on the body."

"Yes."

"How?"

"What do you mean, how? My foot caught on something. I thought it was trash—something that had been left on the dune. Or something that had blown there from the road. I pulled my foot away and then I saw what it was—Jenny Rule's body."

"You knew immediately it was Miss Rule?"

"Of course."

"Why? Were the two of you friends?"

"Not really. I met her first at Marla Norris's home the night of Bea Verdi's murder. And I . . . well, I paid her a visit once at her place."

"What for?"

"A neighborly visit," I said tonelessly.

He smiled, unwrapped the gum, and popped it into his mouth.

My irritation at him was swelling.

"Actually," I admitted, "there was a reason for going to see her. I was making inquiries."

"Oh, is that so?" His grin widened to Jack Nicholson proportions. "How old-fashioned of you, Miss Nestleton. Is that from a play you were in?"

I did my own version of a sardonic grin.

"What were you in-*quir*-ing into, if I might ask."

"Into the murder of Bea Verdi, Detective."

"And who authorized you to make these inquiries?" he said huffily.

"It's a free country, Detective Coop. And in case you've forgotten, I was almost killed in that explosion too. I had every right to ask questions."

"So what did Jenny Rule tell you in response to these inquiries?"

"Nothing," I said.

He stared at me a long time, chewing the gum thoughtfully. "The bell, Miss Nestleton," he said when he finally spoke again. "Tell me about the bell."

"What would you like to know?"

"Did you place it on the corpse?"

"Of course not!"

"Then who did?"

"The murderer, I assume," I replied acidly. "Don't you?"

"What do you make of it—the bell, I mean?"

"I think it's the same kind of bell that was around the neck of that feral cat I saw."

"Yes," he said mockingly, "the mysterious cat of the dunes. The cat that only you can see. The one with the magical mystery bell on its neck."

"It exists," I said simply. "It's no ghost."

"Sure. Whatever you say, Miss Nestleton. But tell me, did the bell disturb you when you saw it on Jenny Rule's neck tonight?"

"Very much so. I took it as an intensification of a threat. First my house was trashed. Now they're saying that I am the next one to die."

"But why would anyone out here want to kill you?"

"Probably because of those inquiries you find so amusing," I said.

"But you said the inquiries yielded nothing."

"That's true. Maybe they are worried that sooner or later my questions are going to yield something."

"Do you have any idea who these people are—the ones trying to get you?"

"No."

"Doesn't it sound ridiculous to you that someone would kill Jenny Rule just as a warning to you?"

"Ridiculous? No. Quite logical. Or rather, it is quite logical that she was murdered in a place where I would find her. As for the real reason she was murdered, I haven't the slightest idea."

Detective Coop stood. "Well, I'll be going now, Miss Nestleton." He went over to the door but didn't walk out. He seemed to be formulating something in his head.

Then he turned back to me. "By the way, you seem to have developed a fondness for one of the local lads, Nick Frye. Is that true, or have I been misinformed?"

I was silent—and embarrassed.

He smiled again, quite lewdly this time. But in a minute the grin turned sad, almost as if he pitied me. At last, he walked out.

I reached out to Bushy in order to hug him. But he abandoned me, leaping quickly off the sofa.

I sat there gloomily. That poor woman. Jenny had been so depressed when I'd visited her. And she had had a premonition of death. What was that dream she had recounted? That snow was falling, lovely white flakes, and each one was the soul of a person long dead.

But wait—was it Jenny who had told me that dream, or was it someone else? I couldn't recall.

Pancho flew by me. Bushy curled up near the door. Everything was now quiet and muted.

I had to shower and go to bed.

But all I did was close my eyes and go to sleep, right there and then.

When I opened my eyes, Bushy was on the sofa next to me, complaining quietly.

The morning sun flooded the beach house.

It took me a full thirty seconds to recall the events of the night before. It took me a few seconds more to realize that someone was knocking at the front door—and it was the knocking that had awakened me.

And it took me even more time to get up from the sofa and hobble to the door, because my whole body had stiffened up from sleeping in such an uncommon bed.

What a silly life, I thought as I swung the door open. Corpses, corpses, and more corpses. And then I felt incredibly chagrined at making light of such horrors. But in a sense I was giddy, almost drunk from the dune activities of the night before and the interrogation by Coop.

Three visitors stood in the doorway: Marla Norris, Lillian Arkavy, and Karl Drabek.

"You poor thing," Marla exclaimed, taking my hand and squeezing it.

Then they all three marched in.

"Sit down! Sit down! You look exhausted," Lillian said.

They pushed me back down on the sofa. Each of them was carrying a gift. Marla had a huge thermos of fresh coffee. Lillian had pieces of fruit in a bowl, most of it squat pears. And Karl had croissants and muffins.

They formed a semicircle around me.

"We heard about the tragedy," Marla said, "early this morning. But we couldn't get details. All we heard was that Jenny was murdered and you found the body."

She thrust a thermos cup of coffee into my hands. I drank. It was bad.

"Yes, it was terrible," I agreed.

"Tell us," Karl urged. He had dropped the bread on the coffee table and was running both his hands over his bald head.

Marla selected one of the croissants, broke it in half, and gave it to me. They were treating me like an invalid.

"What really happened?" she asked.

I held a piece of croissant in my hand, nibbled at it. Then I said, "The cats have to be fed."

Lillian told Karl, "Why don't you just go into the kitchen and feed the cats for Alice."

He looked confused. He didn't move. But he stopped running his hands over his head.

"Did you hear me?"

"Don't give me orders!" Karl replied.

Lillian threw up her hands in disgust and rolled her eyes. "In my opinion," she said, "men have two functions in life. And one of them is to put out the garbage."

"You've written enough garbage to know," Karl retorted nastily.

Lillian slapped him hard in the face.

The slap sounded like an explosion. Everyone startled. Everyone stared at everyone else. No one knew what to say or how to respond.

Finally I said, "Let me feed the cats."

I started to get up. Marla pushed me back down. "I'll feed them," she said, and went into the kitchen.

Lillian and Karl glared at each other but there was no further violence. Marla wrestled the cans open and spooned food into the dishes.

"I'm giving your beautiful cat some turkey," she called out, "and the crazy one some salmon."

From the sofa, I could see my cats staring at me with some suspicion, but little regret.

"You pack a wallop," Karl said, laughing.

"Some novelists do," Lillian replied. But it was not in the way of an apology.

Marla came back. She touched Karl gently on the shoulder, for just a moment. It was Marla's way, I suppose, to tell him that Lillian had just lost control for a moment and she should be forgiven, for these were extraordinary times.

"Now tell us, Alice," Marla urged.

"I couldn't sleep. I took a walk in the dunes. I stumbled on a body. It was Jenny Rule. She'd been shot to death and was just lying on the sand in her nightgown. I remember it had a bow in front."

"Yes," Lillian said. "I know the gown."

"And the killer had left a tiny bell . . . right here." I pointed to the hollow of my neck.

"A bell? Why?" Drabek asked.

"I don't know."

"Did you ring the bell?" Marla asked, crazily. It was a comment as inappropriate as Lillian's slap.

And once again, we all fell silent.

Suddenly, from the kitchen, a gray blur emerged. Pancho dashed across the room, through Lillian's legs, onto the sofa behind my head, down the far side, and back into the kitchen. He scared my visitors half to death. "What the hell is that about?" Karl asked.

"He's grown tired of salmon," I speculated.

"What did the police say?" Marla asked.

"Not much."

"Are they suspicious of you?"

"To some extent."

Marla offered me more coffee. I refused. Lillian took a cup. Karl ate half a muffin. I hoped they would leave shortly.

"Who'll be next?" Lillian whispered.

"What an idiotic question," Karl noted.

"Why? Bea was blown to bits. Jenny has been shot to death. Or are these fantasies?" Lillian replied.

"The problem I have," Marla said, "is that one third of the entire population of our little reading group has now been violently extinguished. Once there were six, including you, Alice, and now there are four. I can't tell you how strange I think this is."

"One third? Why not twelve sixteenths? Or five eighths?" Karl remarked contemptuously. "Sometimes, Marla, your comments are ridiculous."

I winced, hoping he would not be slapped again.

Marla responded, "Why don't you just go home, Karl, and slop some more paint on one of those stupid canvases."

"Sure. I'll do that. But first why don't you give me your

shoes to hock so I can buy some canvases. After all, you're about the only woman left who spends five hundred dollars on a pair of walking-around slippers."

"You have more money than God," Marla snapped back.

A brief verbal fight ensued. I listened with fascination. The realization was beginning to dawn on me that I didn't have the slightest inkling what these people were all about. And I surely didn't have a clue to the real relationships that existed between them. After all, Marla had never disclosed to me that she and Bea Verdi had been close friends at one time. What else were they hiding?

When the fight was over, Lillian began to speak with love of Jenny Rule. Marla wept. Karl began to pace back and forth. My cats seated themselves just outside the perimeter and began their postmeal cleaning. They seemed to be curious about my visitors.

When Lillian had finished what was essentially a graveyard oration, Karl Drabek said with great feeling, "The world's horrors have been visited upon Hollandia."

Then they all left.

What happened next was one of the most inexplicable series of events in my life.

I will try to be calm and analytical in the recounting.

After they left I took a shower, tidied the house a bit, and climbed into my own bed for a few hours of sleep.

I fell off immediately. And I dreamed.

Marla, Karl, and Lillian were walking at night on the dunes. They were wearing what looked like white space suits. Each of them had a bell around his or her neck. As they walked, the bells rang out a light tinkling version of "Row, Row, Row Your Boat."

They came upon a cat lying at the bottom of one of the dunes. It was a large lynx—a bobcat with ferocious tufted ears.

The cat was alive but exhausted. She had just given birth to a litter. The babies were, alas, stillborn.

Lillian said, "Hush the bells."

All three grasped the bells around their necks so that they were silent.

Karl pointed to one of the dead kittens and said, "I told you so."

They all knelt.

The kitten Karl had pointed to had the face of Alice Nestleton.

That was the dream. I woke with a scream. The moment my face appeared in the dream, I woke up. Every part of me was trembling.

Right then and there, immediately upon awakening, I knew that if I did not leave Hollandia immediately, I would be murdered.

Gone was my brave resolve after the house had been trashed as a threat. Gone was every iota of bravery and sang froid I had ever possessed or exhibited in the face of danger.

I had to get out of that place.

I pulled my valise out of the closet and began to pack. Then I called the number of the jitney to New York and reserved a space on the late-night run back into Manhattan. Leaving Hollandia at ten o'clock.

My panic was so great that I couldn't even pack properly. I just kept wandering about the dune house, trying to fathom which objects were mine and which were the owner's of the dune house.

My cats watched me, totally bewildered.

Finally, the bags were packed. I looked at the clock. It was going on six.

Something else was bothering me. A good-bye. I had to say a good-bye to poor Nick Frye. Yes, he would be in another spiral of depression and suicide after hearing of Jenny Rule's death. I didn't know why it would affect him, but I knew it was going to.

Yes . . . I had to say good-bye to young Nick Frye.

Where would he be now? At his tacky little shack, coiling a rope? On the dunes with the old man?

No. He would be drinking with the rest of the locals in one of those bars in town.

I left the house without any qualms and started the long walk into the village. The day grew dark and there were drops of rain.

Oh, what a long walk it was, but I felt strong and oddly happy.

By the time I reached the village it was pitch dark and the rain was coming down heavily.

There were only two local bars; the others were for the summer people.

He wasn't in the first one.

The second one—whose windows fronted the main street

but whose exit was on the side street—was packed with locals.

I edged my way along the bar. No one paid me any mind. He wasn't at the bar.

My eyes grew accustomed to the gloom. I ordered a stein of ale. Then I wheeled on the bar stool and surveyed the booths in the rear.

Yes. He was there. In a booth. With four or five other people.

Seated next to him, close, was Marge Towski.

I sipped the ale and watched him. The child was glum. The others were talking and laughing. He was just staring straight ahead.

I started to walk toward the booth.

But suddenly Nick Frye turned in his seat and buried his face in Marge Towski's hair.

I stopped in my tracks. My heart almost burst at seeing him in such despair.

And then I felt pain and horror and regret and disappointment. And hatred for Marge. It was clear to me then that Marge had been Nick's girl until Bea had fragmented them.

But it was *my* hair he should have been embracing. He should have been turning to me . . . to take care of him . . . to ease his pain.

And then I turned around and ran out of the bar in the driving rain.

I walked steadily toward the house. I was oblivious to the rain. I was walking the way my grandmother used to walk when she was called to the barn on a rainy night for any one of the hundreds of crises that could happen on a working dairy farm.

When I reached the house I walked inside, drenched, and stared at the valises standing fully packed in the center of the living room.

My cats were carrying on. I had forgotten to feed them their evening meal. I began to laugh.

"Bushy," I said, "you have no idea what a first-class dope I've been."

I fed them and unpacked. I was so ashamed of my temporary insanity, of my fear as well as my infatuation, that I went to bed that night without brushing my hair, because I couldn't bear to look at such a foolish face.

No dream was going to drive me out of Hollandia before my time. No dream, no person, no thing.

The next morning I calmly made breakfast and reflected on how I would proceed if I were back in my normal milieu.

What would be my next step? It was not the first double murder I had ever encountered.

But was it a double murder? Perhaps not. Perhaps it was simply two unrelated murders. But then again, if *I* turned out to be the third corpse, it had to be a triple murder. I giggled a bit hysterically and made myself another piece of toast and inundated it with butter and jam. Plenty of jam.

After consuming two more pieces of toast I walked outside into the morning sun with my coffee. Someone waved to me; it was Marla Norris. I waved back to her. She started walking toward the beach. Then she stopped and waved to someone else, someone coming from the beach and toward the dunes.

It was Dayton Coop. He approached to within about five feet of her. They seemed to be speaking. I wondered if he had noticed me from that distance.

Then they started to walk together, very slowly, toward the ocean. Now it seemed Marla was simply listening, with her head down as she walked. From time to time the detective moved one arm as if he were emphasizing a point.

I wondered what he was talking about. No, I knew what he was talking about. He was probably recounting what his local informants had told him; how the strange house sitter had wandered into the local bar during a rainstorm and made an ass of herself.

Yes, and he was probably pumping her with questions about me. Who is this Alice Nestleton? Is she really just a house sitter? What about visitors? Friends? What the hell is going on with that lady?

I drained the cup and walked back into the house. The whole house was lit by the sun. It was glorious. I whirled around in a creaky pirouette, gathering Bushy's attention.

Then I stood still and lifted my arms skyward. Like a votary to the sun. Then I burst out laughing. I was acting so absurdly. As Karl Drabek had said—sand, surf, sun. It was intoxicating in the spring.

Go, Cat Woman, go! I urged myself.

I got down to business. The first order of business being to show somehow that the murders were related.

How did I know that? I felt it very strongly. Maybe the

connection was only mystical, at this point. Before one murder I had seen the dune cat. And before the other, later murder I had heard the dune cat. But a connection was a connection.

Now to find the core, the nitty-gritty, the steak not the sizzle . . . the real connection between Bea Verdi and Jenny Rule in life and in death.

Think, Alice, think. Bushy was thinking. He had curled up—that usually meant deep thought.

Bea was young. Jenny was old. Bea was beautiful. Jenny was way past the age when the conventional standards of beauty could be applied.

Bea was a poet masquerading as a famous poet. Jenny didn't seem to give a damn—she had a private life.

If it was a double murder there had to be a commonality between their apparently disparate lives.

A hobby? A vocation? A great hate? What? I really didn't know enough about them. On the face of it there was absolutely nothing.

My head was bloody blank. It was so blank I began to recite my recipe mantra. Let me explain about this.

I once had an acting coach I respected professionally. This teacher gave me an assignment: to select and prepare a dramatic monologue that best defined me. As a joke I found one of my grandmother's old recipes and recited it in class.

"Pancakes for about four people:

"Put in a mixing bowl half cup milk . . . two tablespoons melted butter . . . one egg.

"Beat lightly.

"Sift one cup flour . . . two teaspoons baking soda . . . two tablespoons sugar . . . half teaspoon salt.

"Add to milk mixture all at once. Stir only enough to dampen the flour. Add more milk if necessary to make batter about the consistency of heavy cream."

That was the piece I did for the class. He was enraged. He threw me out.

Anyway, ever since that unfortunate incident, I have used the pancake mantra as both a warm-up before an acting performance and as a way to break through mind blocks. When I have to think and can't, I start reciting that damn pancake recipe.

Sometimes it works and sometimes it doesn't. That morning it didn't. I couldn't imagine a connection between the two women—either dead or alive—other than the fact that they both lived in beach houses in the Hollandia dunes.

It was time, I realized, to take a walk, to clear up my dimwittedness. I left the house and headed toward the general store to pick up the mail.

What a difference a few weeks made. When I first arrived in Hollandia I had a feeling of acceptance . . . the dunes seemed to wrap me in a kind of security. One could recover in all this solitude from whatever ailed one.

But now all that was changed. I walked differently. Not only had I made a fool of myself in the interim, but I was now walking on deserted roads in a place where someone had made quite clear his or her desire to kill me. What else could have been the meaning of that bell on Jenny's throat? Yes, it was a bitter difference. I walked boldly, trying not to let it get to me, but the boldness was a sham. I was furtive. I watched my back and my front. Small movements in the sky or on the ground—birds or squirrels—made me start.

When I reached the small post office attached to the general store there was only one item waiting for me. It was a letter from Tony Basillio. I sat down on the small bench outside the store, just to the right of the gas pumps, ripped open the envelope, and read the letter.

"Dear Swede,

"Haven't you had enough of that nonsense? I know you'll be back after Memorial Day but I think you should pack the whole stupid thing up right now and get back to me. How much solitude can a person bear? You sound from your postcards like you're going around the bend. By the way, stop sending me those damn cards. Either call or write a real letter or do nothing. Got it?"

I looked up at the sky, grinning. Tony's letters were always disjointed, ungrammatical, and made no sense whatsoever. He alternately begged, ordered, pleaded, distorted. But it was very good to hear from him.

I continued reading the very imperfectly typed script.

"I'm getting very depressed, Swede, with you out there on that beautiful beach and me back in the city. I'm getting so depressed I can't even look for work and I have eleven dollars left and I'm thinking of trying to remember what you got in your loft so I can steal it and hock it. I figure you'll never know.

"The way I see it, you are staying out there deliberately in order to torment me. I am truly beginning to believe that you are out to stultify, to hinder, to set roadblocks up against the free and delicious outpouring of my theatrical genius. I accuse you of orchestrating a massive conspiracy, in addition, making sure that no producers will hire the most sublime and innovative stage designer since . . . well . . . you get the picture.

"Of course, I will take back all the charges if you immediately call me and say you'll meet me for a night of love in some dinky motel halfway between Hollandia and Manhattan . . . on your credit card, of course.

"Now . . . let's get down to business. Sexual deprivation. You have in the past accused me of being a philanderer . . . and there is no doubt that there may have been instances of deviation on my part.

"But that is all over. I long for you. I wait for you.

"By the way, let me give you just an inkling as to how faithful I am now.

"Do you remember De Wilde Brett, the producer with the funny name and the big stomach? Of course you do. Well, he invited me to one of his parties a few days ago, in Tribeca.

"I went. Nothing but wall-to-wall beautiful young actresses. And they kept staring at me. I could read their minds. Who is this handsome well-dressed utterly cool middle-aged dude? Yeah . . . they were checking me out.

"And then they began to proposition me. One, two, five, ten of these luscious things asked me to take them home and maybe come up and have a bite to eat. Well, I was tempted, Swede. After all, I'm alone. You left me alone like a dog. But then I thought of you and I spurned them all.

"As I was leaving, I was literally attacked by the star of the second-highest-grossing off-Broadway musical. Yep, Swede, it was close. She jumped on me and started ripping my clothes off. But I fought back because I love only you Swede and I'm saving myself for you Swede—and I ran naked into the night."

By this time I was laughing so hard I almost fell off the small bench. He didn't say much more. I folded the letter.

It was funny now . . . his words . . . his making fun of himself. But it hadn't been funny at the time when I found out he was sleeping with another woman. And it had precipitated the first of many fissures between us. The simple fact is, Tony Basillio is a wonderful, kind, talented, compassionate man, but until the day he dies he will simply want to go to bed with every woman he meets. And if said woman is young and an actress—well, then his desire often goes around the bend.

But, I thought, he's not a lecher. He's not in that category.

I startled myself. Why did I use the word "lecher"?

Suddenly, as I was seated on the bench, a dazzling new red Mercedes sports car screeched to a halt in front of the gas pump.

A young man got out and started to use the self-service pump. His female companion remained in the car. She was now talking to the backseat passenger: an unhappy-looking middle-aged woman who was scrunched up on the very small seat.

The man finished his pumping, went inside to pay, came out again, got into the car, and drove off.

It was obvious to me what I had seen: a young couple with

lots of money looking for a summer place in Hollandia. The woman in the back of the car was a renting agent showing them the terrain and the dwellings available.

I opened the letter again and read the final paragraph.

"Send my regards to Bushy. Tell him there is a lady of the night waiting for him in an alley on Thompson Street if he is so disposed. And tell Pancho I have submitted his résumé to the Guggenheim Foundation. They are opening their grant program to psychotic cats. Maybe after all these years Pancho can get some help. Stay well. Come back quick and safe. Love, Tony."

It was good hearing from him. I went back to the paragraph where he described his adventure at the producer's party. I laughed some more.

Then I became a bit distraught. Why had I even thought of the word "lecher" in relation to Tony?

Then I remembered where I had heard it last. Someone had used it to describe Karl Drabek when I was making inquiries as to whether he had had an affair with Bea Verdi. My inquiry had been in response to Nick's threats against him.

What exactly did the word "lecher" mean? Well, Webster's didn't back me up on it, but I assumed the word came from "leech," and it meant a man who fastens himself to a woman like a leech for sexual reasons . . . a man whose only purpose in life is to obtain sexual gratification . . . a perverse man who "leeches" on women's vulnerabilities for one purpose only.

But it also meant something more to me. It meant a man who tries to seduce inappropriate partners. That is, the man is interested in sex even if the object is younger than his daughter or older than his mother, a thoroughgoing pervert of eros.

Well, well, well. Something was finally beginning to percolate.

What if Karl Drabek really was a lecher, as someone said? And what if he had really seduced the much younger Bea Verdi? Surely, being a lecher, he would continue his quest for an even more inappropriate object.

What if he had also seduced Jenny Rule? What if that was the connection between the two corpses? They had both, when alive, been the trophies of a lecher.

I got up and began to walk home. I was on edge. The huntress in me was coming out. The sun was almost directly overhead and the day had a slight taste of heat. Honeybees and wasps and bumblebees were haunting the sides of the rows. Braces of swallows zoomed out of nowhere and then back again. There were cars on the road, honking at me as they passed.

I had meant to go straight home but when I saw the top of the Drabek house peeking over the dunes, I stopped.

Wouldn't it be nice to go inside and take a good long look around? I had been there only once, briefly, and acrimoniously. He had basically thrown me out.

I climbed the dune, reached the crest, and stared at the beach house. I could see Karl inside; he seemed to be gathering his things.

I waited. Five minutes later he emerged, carrying canvas and a wooden box of paints along with a large palette. He headed slowly toward the beach. So, Karl was going to play the painter-on-the-beach game. Maybe that was the way he initiated his lecherous embroglios—setting out traps like lobster fishermen.

I stared at the retreating figure. I stared at the house. I circled in place, trying to see if anyone was watching me. Breaking and entering was not my usual mode of behavior. But this was different. I had no friends here and little time. And I was under a possibly delusional, possibly real threat of assassination.

Anyway, this wouldn't really be breaking and entering, because, by tradition, no one locked his doors until the summer people arrived. And then doors were locked not because of fear of theft or mayhem but simply because the beach parties of the summer people always sent forth drunks who wandered into the wrong house by mistake.

I slid down the dune, walked quickly to the house, opened the door, and slipped inside, closing the door softly behind me.

It was as I remembered it—one half of the house his studio, the other his haphazard living quarters.

I went through the living quarters first, opening file drawers, going over and under his ancient sofa, sifting through all his clothes, shaking out all the papers. I was looking for anything that would connect him to both Bea and Jenny. Anything, in any mode.

There was nothing. I stopped, took a deep breath, and went over the living quarters even more thoroughly . . . opening envelopes and letters, inspecting photographs, going through the books for margin notes and gift inscriptions. Nothing.

Thirty minutes had passed. I could not stay much longer. Anything could happen on the beach to send Karl Drabek back to his house.

I walked to the studio side and began to look in all the chests and boxes and behind all the canvases.

I found nothing. There was one stand-up closet in the studio space. I opened it and saw three full duffel bags. Inside the bags were oily rags and brushes and some tools.

Was there an attic? Or a crawl space? If there was, it wasn't visible to me. Besides, there was no more time. I had to get out of there.

But my hands were covered with dirt and dust from the search. They were incredibly filthy. I rushed into the small bathroom and washed them in the sink. Then I dried them on a towel hanging from a rack.

As I started out of the bathroom I noticed a small framed painting on the back of the bathroom door. It was both stunning and strange. Two young people passionately entwined on a sand dune with the ocean in the foreground. The figures were naked. The strangest part of the painting was that it was done in two styles. The right side of the work was in the typical hyperrealist style of Drabek. But the left side of the painting—from the waists to the heads of the two figures— was done in a kind of Chagall-like dream style.

In other words, each of the figures on the sand moved from one painting style to another. Yes, it was quite stunning. So I just stood there and stared.

It wasn't any old sand dune, I realized. And it wasn't any old surf. The dune and the surf in the painting were—when you bracketed out the art styles—vintage Hollandia.

I looked carefully in the lower-right-hand corner of the painting. Yes, there was Karl Drabek's signature. He indeed had painted it.

Did you ever look at a painting or a piece of sculpture or a piece of clothing or even a toaster and at first glance you were totally enamored of said object but as you kept looking you felt that something was very wrong with the object and that not only had you been wrong in your first impression but in some way the object has made a fool of you?

That's what I felt. So I kept peering and turning away and peering. Get out of here, Alice, I kept thinking.

But I kept looking. And then the dominoes began to fall into place. I knew what I was really looking at—a painting of Nick Frye and Marge Towski making love on a Hollandia sand dune.

Or was it Nick and Bea?

That Karl Drabek was most likely a lecher never bothered me. But that he was a voyeur really did disturb me.

More disturbing, inexplicably, was my shock and squeamishness at the fact of Nick and Marge making love in the dunes. Poor Alice Nestleton. Poor pathetic Alice Nestleton. Hadn't I known that all along?

Oh! I wanted to get out of that beach house fast. And I did—running out as if the figures from the painting had leaped off the canvas and were pursuing me. The problems were pursuing me. I was running away from them so fast that I didn't see another person coming in.

Bam!

Our two bodies collided right outside the door.

The next thing I knew, I was sitting up on the ground with my feet stretched out like a little girl in a sandbox.

Across from me was a person seated in the exact same fashion.

But it wasn't Karl Drabek. It was Lillian Arkavy.

What she had been carrying was now on the ground between us. A baking dish with some kind of veal stew and tomatoes, now overturned. A book of Edmund Spenser's poetry, now blotched with tomato sauce from the dish.

She said to me calmly, "Is Karl inside?"

"No," I replied, equally calmly.

"Then what were you doing inside?"

"I don't know."

"Really! And why did you come flying out of there like a lunatic?"

"I don't know."

"Look what you did!" she said, gesturing to the fallen objects.

"I'm very sorry."

"You can't just go in and out of houses around here."

"I realize that."

"Are you hurt?"

"I don't think so. And you?"

She rotated both her arms. She lifted one leg and then the other, trying them out. Nothing seemed to be broken.

My senses came back to me. I realized I was now staring at the spilled objects between us just as I had been staring, minutes earlier, at the painting on the bathroom door.

And believe me, those objects were just as strange.

Lillian caught the gaze on my face. She read it correctly.

"What are you looking at?" she demanded.

I pointed to the overturned stew dish. "Just a few days ago you slapped Karl Drabek in the face. It was obvious to everyone that you hated the man. Why would you be cooking for him?"

"That's none of your business."

Then I pointed to the volume of Spenser's poetry, now bright red with tomato sauce.

"Why would you bring Karl Drabek such a book? Wasn't Bea Verdi's last poem . . . the one she recited that terrible night . . . the one you all mocked . . . a variation on a Spenser poem?"

"Maybe you ought to write a novel," Lillian said with contempt. Then she began to gather her possessions.

I stood up and started to walk away. She called out, "Do you know what I think you ought to do, Alice Nestleton? I think you ought to get out of Hollandia now. We don't want your kind here."

I stopped, turned, and asked bitterly, "What kind is that, Lillian?"

"An angel of death."

I was too flustered to retort. I headed back to my house.

On the way I saw that local trio having one of their dune powwows.

They were crouched together on the ocean slope of a dune: old Harry Bulton, Nick, and Marge.

They weren't speaking. Harry was playing with a stick, making furrows in the packed sand; the two young people were watching him, as if what he was doing was significant.

They spotted me looking at them. They didn't wave. They didn't comment to each other. They just kept looking at me as if I were some kind of migrating bird. That didn't disturb me. As long as said bird was not a surrogate for the angel of death.

That same afternoon, a thunderstorm arrived.

At four o'clock in the afternoon (isn't that the time firing squads go to work?) I was seated on the sofa, drinking brandy.

Now, I try not to drink in the afternoon. But the circumstances were rather unusual.

After all, I had discovered that at least one of my neighbors in Hollandia considered me the angel of death. Worse, my first really disciplined and logical inquiry into the murder of Bea and Jenny had turned out absurd. I hadn't made any connection whatever between them. All I had uncovered was a whole new can of worms. Nay—several cans of worms. None of them explicable except as worms.

And there was this storm. I am afraid of lightning, like all intelligent raised-on-a-farm people. In the countryside, lightning kills people, animals, farms. But neither in rural Minnesota nor in downtown Manhattan had I ever experienced a lightning storm of such intensity.

Maybe because the house was next to the ocean. Or maybe because I had never stayed in a house with so much glass. Whatever the reason, it took brandy and resolve not to shut myself into a closet until the storm was over.

So I sat on the sofa with Bushy beside me, both of us trembling as the crash of thunder and bolts of sizzling lightning alternately shook and illuminated the beach house.

What about dear Pancho? Well, he was his usual inexplicable self.

Just as he had totally changed character when real enemies showed up and trashed the house, so too now he had ceased fleeing.

He was seated calmly right smack in the center of the living room, staring up at the shuddering explosions visible through the glass roof. He was more than calm. He seemed to be watching in a detached academic mode, as if he were about to take notes on the phenomenon, as if he were measuring the intensity.

The storm ended as abruptly as it had begun. And the sun came out brilliantly.

In celebration, I took out Tony's letter and read to my cats the passages relating to them.

Bushy's response was to move as far away as possible on the sofa. He obviously wasn't interested in a relationship with a promiscuous alley cat on Thompson Street.

As for Pancho, I don't think he even heard what I was reading, because the minute the storm stopped, he began his perpetual dash to safety.

I dropped the letter on the sofa. I finished the brandy.

Then I burst into laughter because it seemed so ridiculous that I always ended up on this damn sofa staring up at the sky through the glass ceiling and wondering what I should do next.

"Well, children," I said, addressing any of my cats who cared to listen, "what do I do next?"

Children?

Why did I call them that? It astonished me.

I had never called them my *children* before. I didn't think of them as my children. Bushy and Pancho were my friends, my roommates, my confidants, my sources of strength, mystery, and wisdom. All that and more. All that and more.

But children? No.

What was going on?

What was this new obsession of mine with mothering?

Was it because this house and this place had exacerbated my loneliness?

Was it because of that strange bond I had felt with young Nick Frye and the almost overwhelming desire I had to help him, heal him, watch over him?

Was it because I knew now my life was at risk and I wanted to be among family—even if it was a feline one?

Or was it a return, after all these years, of the dreadful longing I had had as an adolescent to have known and loved and been loved by my mother? To have remembered her face and her touch? It was a longing that was doomed, because the four-year-old mind—the age I was when my parents died—simply could not pass that information on. The memory was buried.

I stood up suddenly, trembling.

The photo! Had I brought the photo? Had I brought the photo of my parents taken only three months before the accident? My grandmother had given it to me when I left her house to take my first acting job at the Tyrone Guthrie Theater in Minneapolis.

I rushed over to my personal papers folder—a pathetic old case fastened by a rubber band. The photo was there. I fished it out and went back to the sofa.

It was such a small photo—glass-framed with cardboard backing.

I stared as I always did, in bewilderment, at the two figures demurely holding hands in front of a tiny frame house. My father wore a white shirt open at the collar. My mother wore a sweater and slacks. It was not a color photograph. It was not a well-done portrait. But what did that matter? I didn't know these people. I ran my hand over my mother's face. I didn't know her! I loved her, but who was I loving?

Quickly, almost violently, I turned the photo over, on the sofa, covering Tony's letter.

Bushy, curled up on the other end of the sofa, was now staring.

"I'm acting strange, aren't I, old friend? Well, Mother's Day is coming. Maybe it's that."

I leaned back and closed my eyes. I heard Bushy climb down from the sofa. I opened my eyes. He was now directly in front of me.

"What's up with you?" I asked. "It's too early to eat."

He started to pace. Maine coon cats are beautiful, but they

do have a kind of clunky pace, compared with Siamese, for example.

"You getting impatient, Bushy? You want me to take the bull by the horns?"

What a stupid expression that was. How do you take a bull by the horns and not end up impaled?

"But Bushy . . . I already took the bull by the horns this morning. Don't you understand? I calmly committed a felony. Breaking and entering. And the only thing I found in Karl Drabek's house just muddied the waters more. And then, when leaving the scene of the crime, I nearly put myself and Lillian Arkavy in the hospital. And she was carrying veal stew and Edmund Spenser to a lecher. Which turned the muddy water into pure sledge. Don't tell me about taking the bull by the horns!"

Bushy was impressed. He stopped pacing. Panch zoomed past, stopped for a moment to say hello with his half a tail, then zoomed onward.

"You and Pancho have nothing to worry about, Bushy. If I become the third corpse in the dunes, Tony will take care of you. You may not think much of him, but believe me, he'll feed you a whole lot better than I do. He'll give you whole ruffed grouse."

No, taking the bull by the horns was not the way to proceed. And I had no desire to recite the pancake mantra again to activate my dormant intellect.

But I had to do something.

If logic hadn't worked . . . if I had been unable to make a

Chapter 8

t was six o'clock in the morning. I was seated on the ocean side of a dune, a hundred yards or so south of my house. The morning was gloomy and windy.

I watched the early-morning runners, joggers, and walkers. Some I had seen many times before; some were new.

I smiled when I saw the couple I called the two stooges. They were truly lovable. The human jogger was an old man who moved quickly enough but as if every step would be his last. He was followed by an old waddling female corgi who could never keep up, or chose not to keep up. Every twenty yards or so the gasping man would stop, turn around, and berate the dog for going so slowly.

Yes, they were a glorious couple.

But I was waiting for Marla Norris, who didn't often jog or run but always took a morning walk along the surf in one of her chic sporting outfits or jogger suits.

logical connection between the two murders . . . why not try illogic?

In my bizarre state it was an overpoweringly attractive thesis.

Like casting a chubby old woman as Helen of Troy.

I giggled to myself. What was the most insignificant, petty fact I knew about these two dead women?

Bea Verdi's fake self-constructed poetic reputation?

No, there had to be something pettier.

What about Jenny Rule's dream of snowflakes?

No. Hardly trivial. Probably at the center of her existence. When she had one.

I needed something absolutely trivial, eccentric, without seeming import, tangential to everything.

Like a mole in the earth I burrowed into the scattered, incomplete profiles of the dead women I had assembled in my mind like surreal collages.

What finally popped out was truly trivial. And truly illogical to focus upon.

Jenny Rule's unpublished pasta cookbook.

I felt ridiculously triumphant. Its irrelevance as the key element in a double-murder investigation was self-evident.

But only misogynists scorn what used to be called "woman's intuition." And that was the only weapon I had left.

She was a bit late that morning, but not much. The minute I saw her I scrambled down the dune and went to intercept her at the waterline.

Marla, that morning, was wearing an exquisite powder-blue satiny jogger suit with a huge unzipped hood flapping in the wind.

She was walking with exaggerated arm movements—a kind of power walk to help increase pulmonary capacity.

"What are you doing on the beach at this hour?" Marla asked, stopping and rotating her arms.

"Waiting for you."

"I'm flattered."

Then I launched into my carefully prepared script. I would have to condense it a bit; Marla looked like she did not wish to tarry.

"I've been thinking about Jenny Rule," I said.

"Haven't we all?"

"I know I'm just a visitor here and I'll be leaving shortly and who knows if I'll ever get back here again on a visit."

I gave one of those acting-school pauses, to make the bait more enticing.

Marla seemed bored by my attempt at cryptic bathos.

"So?"

"Well . . . you know, Marla . . . I met Jenny only two or three times but I thought she was just a glorious person. There was just something so fine about her, and I want to do something."

I was acting up a storm.

"What's there to do? Jenny's dead."

"I mean for her memory."

"A memorial service?"

Then I set the hook in hard and fast.

"No. I mean getting a publisher for her cookbook."

"Are you in publishing also?"

"No. But my niece is living with a wonderful man. Felix is retired, with plenty of money. He spends all his time collecting arcane things. Everything from Victorian garden implements to twelfth-century Chinese sculpture to woven Mexican peasant mats. In fact, he knows so much about so many collectibles that a number of editors in publishing houses who put out guides to collecting this or that use him as a reader or a consultant. Maybe he can give Jenny's manuscript to an editor he knows."

"Pasta cookbooks are hardly arcane," she noted.

"Do you have a copy of the manuscript?"

"Why would I have one? I lived in Italy for five years as a young woman. I know how to cook pasta."

"Where can I get a copy?" I pressed.

"Well," she said a bit testily, "you can't just walk into her house."

It was a rebuke to me, I knew. Obviously Lillian had told her what had happened at Drabek's house. I hoped she hadn't told Karl. That could become uncomfortable.

Then Marla softened.

"It would, I suppose, be a nice gesture if that friend of yours could get Jenny's book published. Why not? Okay. You can probably find a copy in the Hollandia library."

"The library? The book was never published. At least that's what you said. Libraries don't have unpublished manuscripts. At least not small local libraries."

She looked at me as if I were demented.

"Obviously you have never been in the Hollandia library."

"No, I haven't."

"Well, Alice, let me explain something to you about this village called Hollandia. There are more writers here as a percentage of population than in any other place in, probably, the known world. We have famous writers and once-famous writers and near-famous writers. We have novelists, biographers, playwrights, screenwriters, and even people who write the news on Channel Seven."

She started rotating her arms again.

Then she continued, "And there's a tradition in Hollandia of these writers donating their original manuscripts to the library."

"Why?"

"I don't know. Maybe it's just a literary thing. Or maybe . . . well . . . who knows. But they do. And there are some pretty valuable manuscripts there. Probably worth a lot of money, like James Jones's original typescript of *From Here to Eternity*. You do know he used to live near Hollandia?"

"No."

"Well, he did. In fact he died here."

"Where is the library, Marla?"

"Right on the main street. Between the liquor store and the hardware store."

"Thank you."

She was off with a wave. I watched her power walk. She looked like a blue bird who had stepped out of a Bloomingdale's catalog, her feathery hood flapping in the wind, like a crest.

I found the public library quickly. It opened at ten. The liquor store and the hardware store, bookending the library, were already open. I could see someone inside, getting ready.

It seemed astonishing to me that such a wealthy, literate community would have such a small storefront of a library.

But when it opened, twenty minutes later at ten sharp, and I walked through the old swinging doors, I realized you can't tell a book by its cover. Because the library was extremely deep and seemed to have expanded in successive additions toward the rear.

The chairs and tables and card catalogs were extremely old, all made of oak, but the walls were exquisitely paneled and the lighting was superb.

The librarian and I were the only ones in the library that morning. He just nodded to me. I walked slowly along the shelves. He busied himself with some kind of document behind a long low desk.

I gave him a few more minutes to settle down and then I walked boldly to the desk.

He was a strange-looking man, thin and very tall with slouching shoulders, a bright white shirt open at the neck, and thick gray hair parted in the middle.

He wore a name tag over his shirt pocket: Albert Wohl. I had never seen him before and I never saw him again.

"Good morning!" I said.

He looked up at me, a bit suspiciously. He nodded.

"I would like to look at a manuscript a local writer donated to the library. I understand it is a custom here."

He pushed his chair a bit away from the desk, clasped his hands behind his neck, and regarded me—how shall I put it?—critically.

Then he asked, "Who are you?"

"Alice Nestleton," I replied. "I've been staying at the Littleton house on the dunes."

"I know the house," he replied.

There was an awkward pause.

He said, "Do you have authorization?"

"Authorization? The woman is dead. It's Jenny Rule's manuscript I want to see. I assume she donated it many years ago."

A shadow flickered across his face. He had known Jenny, obviously, and he knew she had been murdered.

"Why do you want to see it?"

The way he asked the question infuriated me. What was he? A police officer or a librarian? He was acting like the former. Or maybe an armed security guard at a nuclear installation. It was a damned cookbook! That's all. My little "irrelevant fact" seemed to be taking on bigger and bigger implications.

I was sorely tempted, right there and then, to stop this line of inquiry. I mean, how far should one pursue what at the time had been a choice of desperation?

But I didn't. I simply decided to repeat the same mélange

of truth and lies I had told Marla—about my niece's boyfriend, Felix, who might be able to get the book published as a fitting memorial to a wonderful woman.

Albert Wohl listened carefully. He kept shifting in his chair. When I had finished I just stepped back and waited.

It was a long wait. He seemed to be mentally struggling with my story. He seemed very reluctant to let me see the manuscript.

Then I lost my temper.

"What's the problem here, Mr. Wohl? I'm not asking to see a manuscript by a famous writer, so I can steal it and sell it for fifty thousand dollars at auction. I just want to look at an old woman's cookbook. Wasn't that what this whole thing was about? Letting local authors who don't get published put their manuscripts in the library so their neighbors can read them? Am I wrong about that?"

Sometimes you have to gently prod a mature male into being a gentleman. Like lionesses dealing with incompetent male lions who are fouling up the hunting strategy of the pride.

Of course, Mr. Wohl was not an arrogant black-maned lion. He was a gray-maned librarian.

But it worked just the same.

"You are obviously right," he declared. "Why don't you sit down at that table and I'll bring you Jenny Rule's manuscript."

"Thank you."

I sat down. He came to the table five minutes later without the manuscript. Instead he had a single piece of paper, which he laid down on the table in front of me. He handed me a fountain pen.

"Would you sign this, please."

I grabbed the pen and signed it without reading. He vanished.

When he came back the second time he had the manuscript. He placed it on the table and left.

Oh, it was a sad sight: one of those old-fashioned report covers—thick stiff pink plastic—with elaborate fastening devices.

There was a peeling label on the cover. It read:

EAST END DUMPLINGS
by Jenny Rule

That silly woman, Marla Norris, had gotten even the subject matter of Jenny's book wrong. Obviously it was in no way a pasta cookbook.

I opened to the title page and read the full title.

EAST END DUMPLINGS
Traditional dumpling recipes of indigenous fishermen and farmers on the East End of Long Island

It was, as they say, a mouthful, but it gave me a kind of warm glow.

I turned the page to the acknowledgments section and read carefully. Jenny told how she first got interested in the project after reading an article in *Newsday*.

The article described how several students at a private girls' high school in Montauk had formed a Long Island folklore group.

Their first project was to gather old recipes to discover if there was such an animal as a distinctive East End cuisine reflecting the fishermen and farmers who populated that section of Long Island for more than two centuries.

Jenny also paid special tribute to a student in the folklore group who had shared her information. That student's name was Beatrice Toscano.

I didn't read further.

Had I found the connection? Had my wild fling at illogic turned over the key to the murders? Was it possible that Beatrice Toscano was none other than Bea Verdi?

Chapter 9

A week or so passed in repose, getting my "woman's intuition" moved into an action mode.

Then I rented a car.

Did you ever rent a car in Hollandia? I hope not. It is a very bizarre experience.

The tiny rental agency is attached to the old railroad station. It most definitely has nothing to do in any way, shape, or form with one of the national car rental chains like Hertz or Budget or Alamo.

Behind the counter waiting for me that morning was a pale reflective young woman with two long, very long, light brown pigtails falling down over her front.

They were the longest pigtails I had seen in years. They entranced me. I had the desire to yank one of them but, of course, I did nothing of the kind.

As I approached her I also had the feeling that she

couldn't be more than fifteen. But that was impossible, I realized. There are child labor laws even in Hollandia.

"I'm Racquel," she said to me, smiling, sitting up behind her high counter, which contained one PC, a printer, and one telephone.

She sounded like she had gone to class to learn how to deliver such a greeting. Well, I shouldn't make fun of her. After all, I still attend acting classes.

"How may I help you?" she added. Her face was pixieish.

"I have to rent a car."

"What kind of car?"

"I don't know."

"For how long?"

"I don't really know."

"Can I have your credit card?"

I slid the plastic across the counter to her.

"May I see your driver's license?"

I slid that also. She input all the data.

"What is your Hollandia phone number?"

I gave it to her.

"What is your destination?" she asked.

"Why do you ask that?"

"Well, we have many mileage options."

"I have no idea where I'm going," I said, lying for no reason whatsoever—except that I had begun to resent her prying.

"You do understand that you must return the vehicle to this location?"

"Do you have any other locations?"

"No."

"So?"

She pointed her finger past my ear.

"Those are the vehicles we have available now."

I followed her point out the window.

Parked side by side in the train station lot were two beaten-up compact cars. One was maroon, the other white. Both were filthy.

"That's all you have?"

"That's it."

I don't know much about automobiles. Nor do I like any of them particularly. But these were ridiculous.

"I'll take the white one."

She took out a set of keys and began punching the number into the computer. "By the week or by the day?"

"By the day," I said.

"Then you get a hundred miles free and it's seven cents for every mile thereafter. What type of insurance?"

"What's available?"

"Collision or personal liability, or both."

"Do I need it?"

"That's up to you."

"None, then," I said.

She made a face. Then she asked a peculiar question: "Did you buy a house around here?"

"If I had the hundred thousand or so in cash needed for just a down payment on a Hollandia dune house, wouldn't I get insurance?"

Racquel found my answer humorous.

"But if I had the money I probably wouldn't buy out here. It's a cold place."

"It's okay," she said, starting to print the invoice.

I don't know why I asked the next question. But I did. "Are you a local, Racquel?" I used the slang term the summer people use. I really didn't realize it was a derogatory term until I saw her flash a bit of anger at the question.

"I was born here, if that's what you mean."

"Then you know Marge Towski."

"Sure."

"And Nick Frye . . . and that old man Bulton?"

"Yes, I know Nick and Harry."

We stared at each other. She seemed to be waiting for me to take the conversation deeper. And I wanted to, but the thought of bringing up again all those strange feelings I had for young Frye prevented me from saying another word.

She slid the car keys along the counter to me, along with my credit card and driver's license.

I started to walk out.

"Enjoy the car," she said.

I stopped and stared at this pig-tailed child. She was smiling, but without real friendliness. These "locals" were very strange. They seemed so ill at ease, almost as if they were visitors in their own village. The people with money in Hollandia, those who had bought land and built beautiful beach houses, thought the locals to be even duller than they were strange. Even a wild artistic child/man like Nick they considered dull. But they were all wet, those moneybags. These locals were incredibly complex. Their "distance" was an affectation. I knew that. They were like Native Americans who return to an old burial ground to find a shopping center built over it. The only response there can be is confusion.

The car rental girl cocked her head and pulled on one of her pigtails. A silly, fey gesture.

"Did you know there were two murders in Hollandia during the past few weeks?" I asked her.

"Were they reported in the papers?"

"I imagine they were."

"Then I know about them."

A sudden fear flashed through me. This young woman had booby-trapped both of the cars. It didn't matter which door I opened. I would be blown away. Like Bea Verdi.

The fear was groundless.

That dirty white compact performed better than I did. It took me a long time to find Island Grammar even though I had the address of the private school and I had located it on the map, and Montauk was only twenty-six miles from Hollandia as the crow flies.

But I'm not a crow and the moment I left the main east-west road I got lost on one-lane thoroughfares that hadn't even been noted on the map.

By the time I finally located Island Grammar it was early afternoon. I pulled the car into a lovely tree-shaded space and stared at the low red brick building, which was set far back off the road. It wasn't what I had expected. More like one of those suburban post offices set in the back of a mall than a private school for young ladies. Most of the same-sex schools had some religious affiliation, I knew, but there was not a single religious emblem on the building. Well, maybe it's a Quaker school, I thought.

During the last few days of repose I had constructed what I thought would be a simple and effective cover story.

I was a reporter for the daily paper *Newsday*, in which the article about the formation of the folklore group at Island Grammar had originally appeared.

I was visiting the school to do a follow-up. A standard kind of story. Ten years later, what had happened to all those brave young women's aspirations after they got out into the real world? Yes, it was a good cover story. The request for photos of the girls then made sense.

Request for any kind of information on these girls would make sense, given the thrust of the story.

I had also obtained from the original article the name of the folklore group's faculty adviser: Simone Secors.

Yes, I was ready. But I didn't get out of that rental car for a long while. It wasn't that I was scared. No, it wasn't that. Something about the whole adventure was beginning to disturb me. Maybe reason was returning. Maybe I was becoming mistrustful of any investigative breakthroughs based on illogic.

Anyway, when I finally did walk into the school, I didn't get far—just into a small space between the outside doors and the first row of inside swinging doors.

An imposing woman seated on a chair along the wall, with a clipboard in her arms and a silver whistle around her neck, said, with exquisite diction, "Where are you going?"

Obviously the woman was some kind of monitor assigned to the doors.

"I am going to see Simone Secors," I said.

"Do you have an appointment?"

"No."

"What is this in reference to?" She was beginning to look me over suspiciously. I realized I had dressed wrong, wearing that short denim jacket that is twenty years too young for me.

I gave her the reporter cover story.

"Did you say for *Newsday*?"

"Yes."

"Do you have any identification?"

"What kind of identification?"

She laughed. "Something that will identify you as an employee of the newspaper you mentioned."

Now, this was, I suppose, one of those defining moments.

I had absolutely no identification whatsoever on my person. I had no hope of obtaining any such information or fabricating it. My failure to anticipate such a request merely shows you my state of mind.

Yes, it definitely was a defining moment. I reacted elegantly. I did what I had to do. I maneuvered myself out of danger.

How? Quite simply. By somehow, intuitively, reading my audience of one absolutely correctly. Sooner or later twenty years of acting had to pay some dividends.

"They're in the glove compartment of my car," I said

sweetly. "I'll be back in a moment," I added. Then I turned and headed out.

Just as I pushed the outer doors asunder, I heard her call me back. "Just a minute. Forget it. Simone has a class now. Why don't you wait in her office?"

So I went to her office on the second floor. The door was open. I walked right in and sat down on a folding chair. There was another chair behind the desk. The office was painfully small. Just two chairs, a desk, a narrow high bookcase, a file cabinet, a single window, a blackboard leaning against one wall, and a telephone on the desk. There was a large calendar on the wall. It had been flipped to May. And the illustration for May was a full-color photo of a Peruvian Indian climbing a high mountain pass while chewing coca leaves. I wondered if Simone Secors knew her calendar was shilling for narcotics—that's what coca leaves are.

I waited only ten minutes or so. Simone Secors entered saying "Yes? I heard someone was waiting for me." She flung her books savagely down on the desk. Then she apologized. "I'm weary." She set her face into a smile. She was a chunky woman about fifty wearing a knit suit that should have been in mothballs already. Her hair was frizzled all over.

I introduced myself as Lila Nestleton, for fear she was a secret off-Broadway pilgrim and would know the name Alice Nestleton.

Then I gave Simone the same spiel I had given the whistle-blower guarding the doors.

And I finished it with a question: "Are you still the faculty adviser on the folklore group?"

"The folklore group," she repeated, smiling fondly at the memory. She said wistfully, "Not really. The group disbanded about three years ago. None of the students seemed interested anymore. But I think your idea is wonderful. I still get letters from that first group. And I remember the article quite well. What ever happened to the reporter on the original story? He was very good."

"Oh, you mean Dwyer," I lied. "He got a job with a paper in San Diego. I hear he's city editor now."

"Just tell me how I can help you, Miss Nestleton," she said.

"Call me Lila," I said. "What I really need are the current addresses of that first group of girls. And, if possible, their graduation pictures. Then, when I go interview them, I'll ask them for current photos. We'll print the old and new pictures side by side. It ought to be a nice touch."

Her face lit up. "Yes, a very nice touch. Actually you don't need the yearbook photos. If I remember correctly, there was a photo of all the girls in that first group, together. It was shot when I took them to the Riverhead Museum of Long Island History. A wonderful place. Did you know there were seven Indian tribes living on the East End of Long Island when the Europeans first showed up? Anyway, let me try and find that photo. Actually, that Mr. Dwyer, the one who wrote the original article, was going to use that photo but he didn't have the space."

She stood up. "Let me get the photo first, then I'll give you all the addresses I have."

She turned, took one step, opened the file cabinet, and began to rummage through it with passion.

I waited, literally on the edge of my seat.

She pulled out a big manila envelope and emptied the contents on the desk. "Here!" she almost shouted. "Here it is!"

Seven girls and Simone were bunched together in front of an old building with marble pillars.

"We asked a crossing guard to take a photo," she recalled, "so we could all be in it."

"That article," I said softly, "mentioned a Beatrice Toscano as the leading light of the group."

"And she was," Simone agreed, pushing the photo across the desk to me and tapping one spot. "That's her."

I stared down. My God! There was no doubt about it now. The girl in the photo was Bea Verdi. I tried to remain calm. "Can you identify the others?"

"Of course."

She pointed out each face and gave her a name. Then she wrote the names on a piece of paper. She pulled a thick leather book from her desk.

"I'm not sure if all these addresses are current. But they're all I have."

She wrote them down next to each name.

"Where does Beatrice Toscano live now?" I asked innocently.

"Northold. She lives with her mother, who has an antique shop there. I don't have the exact address, but it's a small town."

Why had Bea used the last name Verdi instead of Toscano

when living in Hollandia? Why had she fabricated her career? Why had she claimed she had moved to Hollandia from Manhattan? Why had Jenny Rule covered up those lies?

Was it really all about dumpling recipes?

Simone Secors then extracted a huge paper clamp from her desk, fastened the photo to the name and address sheet, and handed the packet to me.

"I don't want to lose that photograph," she said. "It's dear to me."

"I'll make a copy," I promised, "and get the original back to you as soon as possible."

"The years pass so swiftly when you teach girls," she said.

"I think I'll contact Beatrice Toscano first. Can you tell me how to get to Northold?"

"It's easy," she replied. "Go back to the highway and drive west to Route 114, and take that through Sag Harbor to North Haven. You get the ferry there to Shelter Island. Then drive across the island to the other ferry. That'll take you to Greenport. You have now crossed the Peconic Bay and you're on the North Fork. You are then three miles from Northold, and there are plenty of signs."

"I'm going to do my best on this project," I promised her.

She was glowing like a well-fed cat when I left.

I followed her instructions to the letter, and they were excellent. But it took me more than two hours to get to Northold, because ferries are not crows. These were powerful little boats with ramps for cars and they only left every forty-five minutes. So at both ferry slips I just missed a ferry and had to wait for the next one. I was informed by the ticket seller that after Memorial Day the ferries ran more frequently.

Northold itself was a tiny village with a three-block-long main street. I parked the car at a meter and climbed out to begin my search.

The search ended, however, the moment I exited the car, because directly across the street was TOSCANO on a large store sign.

In fact there were three stores, right next to each other, with the name Toscano over them. There was Nan Toscano, licensed real estate broker. There was Toscano Furniture, specializing in Early American chests and beds. And there was Toscano Antiques—mostly lamps.

I crossed the street. The real estate office and the furniture store were closed.

The antique shop was open. I walked inside. It was a large store for such a small street.

The first thing I noticed was the incredible wealth of inventory. There were small desk lamps and floor lamps. There were hanging lamps, chandeliers, and strange little lanterns. And there were shades of all kinds and shapes. There was a section of Tiffany lamps and a whole wall festooned with Victorian streetlamps.

The next thing I noticed was a cat. A big black cat with white-tipped ears and tail, lying on a beaded cushion and staring at me with curiosity.

"Hello!" I called.

The tail twitched slightly, ever so slightly.

Then a figure came from the rear of the store. She stopped about five feet from me, just behind the cat.

For the longest time I couldn't speak. I had met Bea Verdi only once . . . on the night of her death. And I knew that many mothers and daughters look eerily alike.

But this likeness was uncanny. In form, features, and face, this woman in front of me looked like Bea Verdi made up by a professional makeup artist to be simply an older edition of herself.

She didn't say a word. She waited for me to speak.

I said, "I am so sorry about what happened, Mrs. Toscano."

And then she did a very peculiar thing. She swiftly picked up the black cat and crushed it lovingly to her chest. As if she were protecting it. As if I had come into her shop to harm the cat. As if I were a violent, cruel woman.

And still she did not speak. She no longer looked at me. She focused her eyes on the floor, at a point equidistant between us.

"You are Beatrice Toscano's mother, aren't you? You *are* Bea Verdi's mother."

I don't know why I used both names. I don't know why I phrased the first part as a question and second part as a declaration. I just did.

It didn't matter. She said, "No."

I didn't know what to do next. I mean, the woman was probably still in grief . . . maybe even in denial. But she was Bea's mother. Why was she denying it?

"Please, Mrs. Toscano. I just want to ask you a few—"

She didn't let me finish. "Shut up!" she cried out and let the frightened cat down. "I want you to leave here immediately. If you don't I will start to scream for the police."

I gave out a nervous little laugh. Was this woman insane?

She began to scream. I ran out of the store, crossed the street, and climbed into the rented car. It felt like sanctuary. I fumbled with the ignition keys. My hands were shaking. I couldn't insert the key in the slot. I kept staring across the street, but happily the woman had stayed inside the shop and there were no other screams and no one on the block seemed to have heard the first shriek.

Finally I got the vehicle started and headed back toward the ferry.

After returning the car to the agency, I kept close to the dune house for the next few days. To be quite honest, that shrieking woman in Northold had reawakened my fears of becoming the third corpse. I took long solitary walks along the beach during the hours when no one else was there. I waved to those I knew but did not approach them. I even followed an elaborate, infuriating recipe and baked bread.

But always during those days, finally, I sat back down and studied the photo Simone Secors had given me.

The more I gazed at the lovely Beatrice Toscano, the more frustrated I became. I had uncovered the connection between the two corpses but I could not break through to anything that made sense of the connection. It was still, on the face of it, trivial.

On the fourth day after being driven from Nan Toscano's

antique shop I decided to construct a possible scenario—a play in eleven scenes called *Death in Hollandia*.

I took a yellow legal pad, two ballpoint pens, and a beach chair and went out to an isolated dune. I sat down on the chair, my face to the ocean, and began to compose.

Scene One. Ten years ago. Jenny Rule is intrigued by newspaper article on folklore group in private high school. The intrigue is culinary. Jenny makes contact with student at school, Beatrice Toscano.

Scene Two. Five years ago. Beatrice Toscano moves to Hollandia. She now has a new name—Bea Verdi. And a career as a writer/poet which may or may not be bogus.

Scene Three. Four years ago. Young man named Nick Frye falls in love with Bea Verdi. Follows her around like a puppy dog. Never consummated. Middle-aged lecher/voyeur named Karl Drabek may or may not have pursued Bea also.

Scene Four. The present. Alice Nestleton comes to Hollandia. Finds a happy dune community. Discerns no special relationship between Jenny and Bea . . . between any of the residents.

Scene Five. The present. Alice Nestleton goes to poetry reading. Sees a stray cat with a bell feasting on a dead horseshoe crab before entering the reading. Bea Verdi recites a poem about her beloved old cat, using a Spenser poem as a model. She is critically attacked. She runs out. She is murdered by a booby trap.

Scene Six. The present. Young man, Nick, attempts suicide. Then threatens to murder Karl Drabek. Alice Nestleton starts an investigation out of affection for the young man.

Finds little evidence that Drabek either slept with or murdered Bea Verdi.

Scene Seven. The present. Alice Nestleton's beach house is trashed as some kind of warning.

Scene Eight. The present. Jenny Rule is found shot to death. Tiny feline bell left on corpse to warn Alice she is next.

Scene Nine. The present. Alice intuits a connection between corpses. Sneaks into Drabek's dune house. Finds painting of Nick and Marge Towski making love. Also discovers some kind of strange relationship between Lillian Arkavy and Drabek.

Scene Ten. The present. Alice Nestleton finds original connection between Jenny and Bea. Locates Bea's mother. Hits roadblock.

Scene Eleven. The present?

I put the pen down. It sure was a lousy play. No denouement. Sketchy characters. Key events probably left out. Trivial events probably overemphasized.

I read it over. Why hadn't I put Marla Norris in the play? Or Harry Bulton?

I doodled along the edges of the pad. Why did I keep thinking I was so close to understanding the murders?

I burst out laughing. Why hadn't I put Dayton Coop in the scenario? Surly he would be the easiest to cast.

I sat back and closed my eyes. The sun was strong. The breeze was gentle. The surf was musical.

There was only a little more than two weeks left on my house-sitting contract. I wanted to get back to Manhattan safely, with Bushy and Pancho. But I also wanted a finish for *Death in Hollandia.*

One thing was sure—the best way to proceed was to tell the good detective everything I knew. I went back to the dune house to make the call.

Chapter 10

I made seven calls to the state police barracks in twenty-four hours. Detective Coop didn't answer a single one of them, nor did he return my call.

He just showed up at three o'clock in the afternoon, ignoring the bell and banging on the door like a bill collector.

When I opened the door and saw him, I said nastily, "Don't you return calls? I thought you people were public servants."

"I'm neither of the above," he replied, equally nasty.

"Well, come on in."

"I prefer to stay outside."

"Oh, I get it, Detective Coop," I said. "You think all actresses are promiscuous. You think I'm going to put you in a compromising position."

He didn't reply. He just stared at me.

I moved a bit closer to him and dropped my voice into a sexy, mocking Mae West whisper. "Let me tell you something, honey. Now, you are tall and you are lean and you are macho and you are kind of drop-dead handsome like Clint Eastwood . . . but I find you about as sexually attractive as a moth."

"What do you want?" he asked.

"I have gotten hold of some information that you may find valuable."

"Shoot."

I stepped outside the house, walked past him, turned, and recounted with staccato brevity what I had discovered about Jenny Rule, her cookbook, Bea Toscano/Verdi, the Island Grammar School, and Bea's crazy mother.

Then, leaving him to digest that data, I went back into the house, grabbed the photo, walked back outside, and handed it to him.

He perused the photograph for a long time.

"Yes," he finally said, "that surely is Bea Verdi." He handed the photo back to me. We stood together in an uncomfortable silence.

Then he asked: "So what?"

"So what?" I mimicked him angrily.

"What are you trying to tell me?"

"Three things, Detective. First of all, there was a longtime connection between Jenny Rule and Bea Verdi that no one seemed to know about. Second, it had to be something illicit or otherwise why would Bea have disguised her true identity when she came to Hollandia? And third, this connection, whatever it is, led to the both of them getting murdered."

He lit a cigarette. He squinted at me through the smoke.

"Sure," he said. "A lot of people kill for dumpling recipes."

He was making fun of me but I didn't reply in kind.

"It was a double murder, Detective Coop."

"Let me tell you something, Miss Nestleton. Something about police work. A fundamental truth which I'm sure won't sit well with you. When there is a double murder, there is usually the same MO. Murderers are kind of unimaginative. Joe Blow gets drunk and shoots a kid in a bar. He drives thirty miles, robs a 7-eleven store, and then murders the clerk. Two murders—one gun. That is the way it usually works. In the real world. The murders of Bea Verdi and Jenny Rule were so totally different that a double murder just doesn't make sense. Bea Verdi was booby-trapped. Jenny Rule we now know was shot by a high-powered rifle somewhere else and her body was dragged to the dunes. There's no connection between them."

I hadn't known about Jenny's body being dragged to the dunes. It made me fearful again. It seemed to prove that I had been lured out of my house that night by the tinkling bell so that I could find the body.

"So," he said, "forget the goddam dumpling connection. Besides, I've been out here on the East End for twenty years and I never ate a dumpling except in a Chinese restaurant."

"Did it ever occur to you, Detective, that this murderer might be both shrewd and imaginative?"

"What murderer?"

"In other words, the change in MO for each killing may have been planned because he or she knows how police think."

"You're like a bulldog, Miss Nestleton."

"What do you mean by that?"

"You get something in your jaws and you keep chewing no matter what. No matter how the facts contradict your beliefs."

"Well, tell me, Detective, don't you find it strange that Bea Verdi's mother almost had a nervous breakdown when I showed up?"

"Not really. People who lose children often react crazily. It's a terrible thing."

"Granted. But don't you think it's suspicious that the moment Bea Toscano moved here she changed her name?"

"Maybe she liked opera. Or maybe she married and divorced a man called Verdi but decided to keep her married name."

"Then what about the incestuous behavior of all the people around here—the bitter locals who hunker down in the dunes and the owners of the houses who seem to carry on such twisted, mercurial relationships with one another?"

"You've lost me there. They seem like other people I've met. Nothing more, nothing less."

"Dammit, Detective! What about that bell left on poor Jenny's throat?"

"You sound like you're losing control, Miss Nestleton. Maybe I ought to let you in on a little police secret. We've made no progress whatsoever into the murder of Bea Verdi. But we think we have a handle on the Rule murder."

"What handle?"

"We think it was drug-related."

"That's the most ridiculous thing I ever heard. Jenny Rule into drugs? You must be joking."

"I am not joking. I'm very serious. There was a murder in Quogue about six months ago. Very similar. A woman went for a walk along the beach. Around two in the morning. She came upon a skiff unloading something onto the beach. She was shot to death with a high-powered rifle and her body was dumped out of sight behind some dunes. What had happened was she had stumbled on drug smugglers. Hashish. We think that's what happened to Jenny Rule."

"Drug smugglers in Hollandia?" I said. "Talk about fantasy!"

"It isn't fantasy!" he said sharply. "Over the past five years there has been a major change in drug-smuggling patterns. The South Shore of Long Island is once again a port of entry for illegal substances, like it was during Prohibition. The big ships lay off the shore and small boats take the cargo to the beach. These people don't ask questions. They shoot first."

I shook my head ruefully. "You and I are talking different languages, Detective."

"I'll go along with that, Miss Nestleton. So do me a favor and don't call me again unless you have something concrete. As for your dumpling theory . . . why don't you tell your neighbors about it? They look like they'd spend a whole lot of hours trying to make a fish dumpling last made in 1808."

He strode away, letting his cigarette fall onto the dune, still lit.

I crushed it out with my heel. Maybe, I thought, I *will* tell my neighbors. What do I have to lose?

Chapter 11

What a strange telephone conversation I had with Marla Norris.

"Hello, Marla. It's Alice. I have some news for you that will just curl your toes."

At first there was no reply from the other end. Marla was obviously not used to my breathless-starlet mode of speech. Actually I don't use it often.

"My toes have already been curled," she finally said.

"I have to tell you the news anyway. And I have to tell Lillian and Karl. Please, Marla. Can you get them over to your place? Like a meeting of the dune tenants' association."

"We own . . . we don't rent," Marla said a bit sniffily. "Are you talking about now?"

"Yes. It's only five o'clock, Marla. I could be over at seven. I'll bring some pastries. Believe me, what I have to tell you people is astonishing."

I had now moved from the breathless-starlet role to a middle-aged Dorothy Parkerish lush.

She was thinking. I could heard her thinking over the phone. She was also confused by my sudden desperate desire to socialize with them.

Then I pulled out all the stops. "It's not a good time for me, Marla. Things are falling apart."

It was my poor-little-girl role and she just grumbled. Sisterhood is powerful.

"Of course, come on over, Alice. And forget the damn pastries. I'll call Lillian and Karl."

And that was that.

Two hours later, as I trudged along the beach, I had a brilliant technological fantasy. Imagine a criminal investigator who utilizes only a video camera and a questionnaire. The suspects, maybe even dozens of them, are simply asked a few simple questions. Or told a few simple facts. Their faces are then videotaped as their brains absorb the data. The criminal investigator then simply reviews all the facial expressions and because of her brilliance is able to isolate the expression that most signifies guilt. Ah, it was delightful. Alas, I had no video camera, and no brilliance. The rest of the requirements I had in surplus. I mean the data to distribute.

As I climbed the steps of the dune up to Marla's house, I remembered that this was the spot where I had seen the dune cat, hunkering down next to the dead crab. The remembrance chilled me. I stopped moving. What if, right then, I was in the sights of a high-powered rifle? Was it true that you heard the rifle report after the bullet entered you?

I rushed up the steps and banged on the door.

Marla opened with a broad smile on her face, and she actually kissed me on the cheek.

Lillian and Karl were already there. They greeted me like a long-lost relative. It was obvious that Marla had told them I was cracking up and everyone had to be nice to poor Alice . . . poor house-sitting Alice . . . out of her element in Hollandia.

The moment I sat down, Karl presented me with a glass and then poured in some liquid from a huge pitcher.

"My greatest artistic triumph . . . the margarita," he announced.

"Alice has some astonishing news for us," Marla announced.

They leaned forward in anticipation. I gathered my resources, took a long drink of the margarita, placed it down primly, and said, "Do you remember that legendary pasta cookbook that Jenny Rule wrote? Well, it wasn't a pasta cookbook. It was a dumpling cookbook."

Karl burst out laughing. Marla looked confused. Lillian asked, "Is this the astonishing news?"

Then Marla said, "I could swear that Jenny told me it was a pasta cookbook. Besides, I don't remember her ever making dumplings. What kind of dumplings?"

"Indigenous," I replied.

Karl stopped laughing. He asked in a nasty voice: "What the hell does that mean?"

"It means dumplings made by the original settlers on Long Island. The fishermen and the farmers," I said.

"The 'original settlers' were Indians," Lillian pointed out.

"Maybe," Marla said quickly, "Alice is using the wrong word. Perhaps she means 'cartilaginous'—from the word 'cartilage'—pertaining to indigestible dumplings."

"No," Karl said, picking up on the gentle mockery. "What she really means is 'litigious'—pertaining to lawsuits filed by individuals who died from eating bad dumplings."

"No," interrupted an inspired Lillian. "She means 'vertiginous.' Because people got dizzy from eating those indigenous dumplings."

I smiled. Let them have their fun. I watched their faces. I knew I was in the camp of the enemy. Karl had once thrown me out of his home. Lillian had characterized me as an angel of death. Marla had called me all kinds of a pathetic fool.

Then I said, "Actually, that wasn't the news I wanted to tell you. It was just a taste."

"By all means give us the rest of the feast," demanded Karl, jumping up again with his pitcher of margaritas and refilling my glass.

"I paid a condolence call on Bea Verdi's mother," I said quietly.

They stared at me. With blank faces.

I continued, "Her name is Nan Toscano. She lives on the North Fork, in Northold. Toscano is Bea Verdi's real name."

Their faces stayed blank. Almost set in masks. Their response or lack of it unnerved me.

Raising my voice, I added, "She refused to admit she was Bea's mother. She started screaming. She almost attacked me."

I waited. They looked at each other. Then Lillian said, "So what's your news?"

Marla crossed her legs and sipped her margarita.

"Karl," she said, "do you want to tell Alice why this Nan What's-her-name refused to admit she was Bea's mother?"

"No," he replied. "You tell her."

"Well, Alice, you see, Bea didn't really have a mother. Not any longer. Her mother has been dead for some time."

"For a long time," echoed Lillian.

"She told us that," Karl affirmed. "That was one thing she did talk about."

"Any other startling news?" Marla inquired with dripping sarcasm.

I was stunned by what they said. Absolutely stunned. It's one thing to construct a fictional life for yourself, but it's another thing to state that your mother is dead when that lie is not necessary.

"But you're really just playing games with us, aren't you, Alice Nestleton?" Lillian asked.

"No, Lillian. You've got it wrong," said Marla. "She's not playing games. She really thinks she's Miss Marple."

"I think she thinks she's Sam Spade," Karl said.

"Oh yes," Lillian said. "We've heard all kinds of stories about you. They've been filtering into Hollandia from Manhattan. About how you always get involved in the messiest kinds of things."

"And about how you make charges against people just to besmirch them," said Marla.

"The way I see it, Alice," said Karl, "you're either crazy or evil. I think you're crazy, so it doesn't matter if I confess."

He turned to Marla. "Should I confess?"

"By all means," she replied.

"And by any means necessary," added Lillian.

Karl stood up. "Mea culpa! Mea culpa!' he shouted. Then he dumped the half-full pitcher of margaritas over his head.

Marla and Lillian whooped with glee and applauded.

"Here is the way it happened. First Bea. I baked a plastique dumpling. Then I wired it to the car horn. The moment Bea opened the door I sang the first notes of 'Amazing Grace.' The brilliance of my tone activated the horn. The horn activated the plastique. The dumpling blew Bea to Kingdom Come. As for Jenny, it was much easier, but I had to recruit Lillian and Marla."

"Yes!" Marla yelled. "Yes!"

"I made a tiny dumpling. Then Marla and Lillian made their famous mustard sauce. We called Jenny out of the house, then shook the mustard sauce until it reached critical mass. Then we plopped the dumpling into the sauce and it become a jet-propelled mustard dumpling. The rest is history."

He held out his hands, waiting to be handcuffed.

Lillian held out hers. And so did Marla.

I didn't mind the mocking. What I did mind was the hate in their eyes.

I stood up and walked quickly to the back door. I put my hand on the knob.

Then I hesitated. This was the same scenario as that first

night at Marla's house. I was doing the exact same thing Bea had done. She had opened the same door and walked to her car and her death.

I stepped back. I walked back across the room to the front door and let myself out.

It was drizzling.

As I slogged home through the dunes all I could think of was their hatred. I had never run across this before. Some people like me. Some dislike me. Some people even love me. But hate? No.

The phone was ringing when I walked into the house. It stopped before I could get to it. The answering machine was not connected.

Wearily I shed my wet clothes and put on a huge terry-cloth bathrobe. It was the only item I had purchased for my trip to Hollandia, but for some reason I had simply not worn it before.

I was tired, edgy, anxious, confused. I didn't want to think. I moved from sofa to chair and back again. Then I just walked about, sipping a mug of tea and eating two-week-old soda crackers.

I stared at the clock. It was seventeen minutes past nine.

The phone rang again. I listened to it and watched it, as if it were a stranger who had suddenly shown up in my dune house and I was deciding how to treat it.

The phone kept on ringing. My cats stared at me, inquiring. I picked the phone up.

"Yes?"

"Alice?"

"Yes."

"Ivor."

"Who?"

There was a nervous laugh. "Ivor Littleton."

The name rang a bell, but for a moment I just couldn't place it. Then I realized it was the man for whom I was house sitting.

"Did I get you at a bad time, Miss Nestleton?"

"No, no. I'm sorry. I'm just a bit scatterbrained lately."

"How's the weather out there?"

"Beautiful. Just beautiful." Had I forgotten that it was raining?

"It's nice in Manhattan also."

There was a long pause.

"It's so nice," he said, "that I spilled a drink over a pretty lady's skirt at lunch."

I couldn't follow his logic. And I really wasn't interested. The man was a zillioniare stockbroker. I have nothing against Wall Street professionals, but I also have nothing to say to them. They keep away from off-Broadway theaters.

"I hear there have been some problems out there. A veritable crime wave."

"Yes," I agreed, "but a few murders don't seem to be hurting the real estate market."

"Nothing can hurt Hollandia's real estate market."

"Agreed."

Again there was that funny pause.

"How's the house?" he asked.

"Fine."

"You getting used to your neighbors?"

"Sort of."

"Any beach erosion? Break-ins? Lightning strikes? Psychotic gulls?" He laughed after reciting his litany.

"Everything's quiet," I lied.

"Well, look, Alice. I have some bad news. I'm going to have to ask you to vacate the house two weeks early."

I didn't say anything. Nothing could stun me anymore that evening. I listened as if I were listening to a very boring radio play.

"My sister and her husband had to cut short a vacation in France. He has some business in this area before they go back to California. And my sister just loves the Hollandia house. They're coming back this Sunday. Mother's Day. And I really would appreciate it, Alice, if they could have the house the next day, on Monday. I'm going to be driving them out."

He caught his breath.

"Look, Alice, I'd be happy to take care of a motel bill for you during those two weeks if you can't get back into your Manhattan place now."

"That's not necessary," I said.

"I hope you're not angry at me, Alice. This is a bit much to ask, I realize, on such short notice."

"I'll be out Monday morning," I said.

"Thank you. Just one more thing. On the kitchen wall there's a small list of numbers."

"Yes, I know it."

"Could you do me a favor, and before you leave next

Monday call that Marge Towski number. She's a cleaning girl. Ask her to come Monday about noon for a few hours."

"I kept the house clean," I said, "except for a few wild cocaine parties in which a few of the guests vomited on the quilt."

I heard him catch his breath again, trying to decide if I was joking or not. I thought of Marge Towski. So that was the way she supplemented her probably very meager fruit-stand wages while acting as Nick Frye's nursemaid and lover.

Ivor Littleton decided that I was joking.

"You're a gem, Alice," he said. "Again, thanks for everything. Leave the keys in the refrigerator and the door open."

Then he hung up.

What could I say? What could I do? The show was closing. The gig was over. The game was lost. Totally, irretrievably lost.

I woke up the next morning with a bad headache. Worse than the headache was the fact that I hadn't the foggiest notion what day in the week it was.

I got out of bed, consulted the calendar, discovered it was Friday, then went back to bed despite the disappointed moans of Bushy and Pancho, who were quite sure that the only reason I had gotten out of bed was for their breakfast.

I stared at the sky through the glass ceiling and found it rather difficult to believe that tomorrow would be Saturday, the day after that Mother's Day, and the day after that get-away Monday.

I began to fantasize a story to be printed in the local Hollandia paper: "The Alice Nestleton Traveling Theater Group's current production of *Death in Hollandia* will close two weeks before scheduled.

"Critical reviews have been antagonistic. One reviewer called the script 'totally unresolved.' In addition to the bad reviews, the theater in which the company performs has canceled its lease.

"There has been no word from Miss Nestleton as to whether or not the traditional closing cast party would be held. Miss Nestleton refused to answer any questions concerning the production."

The goofy fantasy made me feel better. I got up and fed my cats. Then I took a long walk on the beach. It was one of those mornings when the smell of salt water was pungent and bracing.

I walked about two miles east and then rested on what was left of an old Army Corps of Engineers breakwater which had been constructed a long time ago to inhibit beach erosion.

That goofy closing notice I had fantasized while in bed kept popping back into my mind. It made me feel good. Sure, it was just whistling "Dixie," but it made me feel real good. It gave me the illusion that I was a strong woman. What does total, abysmal investigative failure mean to an old tried-and-true trouper like me?

As I sat on the rocks, another thought began to percolate. Why not a cast party?

There always is some kind of closing party, even if the damn play runs only two nights—and the Alice Nestleton

Theater Group had been performing in Hollandia since March.

The lovely wind began to blow flecks of sea froth against my face. Suddenly I felt twenty-one again! What a delicious idea!

I would invite everyone. Everyone. The locals I knew, the neighbors, even that Dayton Coop. If they didn't show up, the hell with them. If they did show up, I'd be the best damn host they ever saw. Food. Drink. Laughter. A typical closing party. Dancing through the tragedy.

The moment I got back to the house I picked up the phone and called my friend Nora at her theater-district bistro in Manhattan—Pal Joey.

As usual, she answered the phone with a bark, expecting one of her produce suppliers complaining about late payment. When she realized it was me, she said, "Well, it's about time you picked up the phone and called me."

"I'm leaving Monday, Nora."

"What happened?"

"The owner needs his house back."

"The hell with him, Alice. Squat!"

I laughed. "No, it's time to go. I thought maybe you could drive out here on Sunday morning and get me and the cats back on Monday."

"It would be a pleasure."

"And you'll help me with the party."

"What party?"

"Oh, I'll be giving a little party Sunday afternoon for a few neighbors and some other people."

"You want me to cater it, Alice? I can bring out all the Saturday-night leftovers."

"Thanks, Nora, but I think I want something a little more plebeian. Something raucous."

"I have it, Alice! I'll send one of my kitchen guys down to Katz's on Houston Street and get you forty raucous deli sandwiches. Pastrami. Corned beef. Tongue. Bologna. You can't get any more raucous than that. And we'll have old-fashioned potato salad and pickles and bagels and lox and—"

"That sounds great, Nora. Thank you."

"What about booze, Alice?"

"I have enough money for that. I'll get it here in town."

"Okay. See you Sunday," she said and hung up.

I jumped up, did a few tap steps. There were a lot of lists to make—paper supplies list, booze list, guest list. Yes, I was going to leave Hollandia on a dominant.

Chapter 12

The alarm clock woke me at six o'clock Sunday morning—Mother's Day. I fed the cats. I made the bed. I pulled my hair back severely in a bun and dressed in a morbid muslin smock.

Yes, I thought, staring at myself in the mirror, let Hollandia remember me for what I looked like in the mirror—an ageless, sexless actress from some Swedish film director's minor masterpiece.

Then I got down to work. There wasn't really much time. Nora would probably show up about eleven. All the invitations I had delivered, whether verbal or written, had specified twelve noon. So people would probably start showing up about twelve-thirty. The Hollandia people—the rich ones, anyway—were used to brunch parties. I had even bought the makings for mimosas.

First I moved all the tables to the center of the house. I

piled all the paper plates, utensils, napkins, and other items on the smallest table.

I set up the bar on the next-largest table. There were two bottles of vodka, one of gin, one of Campari, one Jack Daniel's, one Dewars, two bottles of red wine, three bottles of white wine. The soda, beer, and ice cubes remained in the refrigerator for the time being, along with the champagne.

The largest table I left alone. The food platters would go on that one.

I made some other minor adjustments to the house. Then I sat down on the sofa and studied my handiwork.

"Well, cats? What do you think?"

They surely were curious, strutting about, half frightened, half combative. They did not like furniture to be moved.

I stared at the cats. Something about them bothered me. They were so undressed. This was Mother's Day. And this was going to be the best cast party ever thrown in Hollandia. Probably the only one.

"You people are going to have to look better," I called out to them. "Or at least get a costume."

My God! I jumped up. I had completely forgotten what I had purchased for Bushy and Pancho in town on Saturday, when I bought the liquor and paper goods.

In the party store, which was really just an overpriced Woolworth's, I had found some startling packing ribbons. They were thin and satiny and they featured a tiny brass bell at one end. If the ribbon was tied right on a package, or, for all I knew, a pigtail, the tiny bell would hang like a pendant on a necklace. I had bought them for my cats.

Having remembered that I purchased them, I now couldn't remember where I had put them. Finally, I did find the ribbons in a kitchen drawer and after a short chase fitted my two beasts with their elegant new necklaces with the tiny tinkling bells.

Each of them at first tried to claw it off, but they quickly gave up the effort. Maybe they liked the soft musical sounds they now made.

"You look beautiful," I told them.

Yes, I thought, watching them, this was a perfect touch. Hadn't almost everyone in Hollandia thought I was a bit strange for insisting I'd seen a feral cat in the dunes with a bell around its neck? Well, I couldn't prove that I was telling the truth—but at least I was providing not one but two understudies.

Oh yes, my lovely belled cats were the perfect touch.

All chores accomplished, I took out a copy of T. S. Eliot's *The Cocktail Party* and started to read. Don't ask me why.

I dozed off at page three. I woke. I read seven more pages. There might be a role in there for me. I read another page. My, it was getting a bit nasty. How come I had never read this play before? I fell asleep, Bushy's new bell tinkling in my ear. Is there anything more wonderful than a nice morning nap when you know that you'll soon be going home? And I would be home in my lovely West Village loft in less than twenty-four hours. Wouldn't I?

The sound of my own name woke me. Alice. Alice. Alice. Alice. Then I realized it was coming from outside the house. I realized it was Nora. Because who else but Nora would belt out my name like it was a variation on Maria, Maria, Maria, Maria from *West Side Story*.

I flung open the door and there she was . . . effervescent . . . the figure of Shirley MacLaine with the pipes of Ethel Merman.

"I don't have time to talk," she shouted. "I'm on a delivery."

She started to unload the car. I rushed to help her.

"Alice! I forgot to tell you. I also brought a band along."

I was startled. "A band? For this party?"

"Sure. What's a party without music?"

"Where are they?"

She didn't answer me. She didn't have to.

"I'm the band," a voice said from behind the car.

And a man appeared. My God! It was Tony Basillio.

"I play the tuba, bass, tenor sax, vibes, electric guitar, and . . . pinochle."

Oh yes, it was Tony, slouching his tall frame down, wickedly handsome with that perpetual hint of dissoluteness. He was dressed in his typical stage designer style. He had cut his hair, and even though it was only about ten weeks since I'd seen him last, there seemed to be a lot more gray in his black brushed-back hair. He had also put on a few pounds. So much for poverty. I was so happy to see him I didn't even kiss him for fear of letting things get out of hand, right there in the open. That wouldn't have embarrassed Nora, but this was Hollandia.

We got all the food in the house and set the platters on the table. We took the cubes and beer and soda and champagne out of the refrigerator. Then we just sat around and reveled

in each other's company. It was so good to see them again.
They ragged me a lot—about how they were struggling in the
city while I was out here on the Gold Coast with all the beautiful people. I didn't tell them a single thing about what had
been going on in Hollandia. What would have been the point?
We were all going home in a few hours.

Of course, I was tempted—particularly when Tony noticed
the ribbons and tiny bells on the cats and said, "If I had
known it was that kind of party I would have worn my 1976
Petrocelli."

At eleven-thirty Nora said, "Well, Alice, let's get down to
brass tacks. Am I supposed to be a waitress or a guest or a
host at this party?"

"Just enjoy yourself, Nora. Please don't do any work."

It was a stupid thing to say. All restaurateurs are compulsive. Five minutes after the first guest arrived I knew Nora
would start getting in my way—ordering me around, telling me to bring more ice, checking on the liquor supply,
and so on.

Tony asked, "And me, Swede? What do I do?" He was
eyeing me lasciviously.

Nora barked at him, "Why do you keep calling her that
stupid name, Swede?"

Tony ignored her.

"Do you want me to be the coat-check girl?"

"It's too balmy outside for coats," I replied.

"Security? Am I your bouncer, Swede? To get the drunks
out."

"The people out here can hold their liquor," I said, then

realized it was not exactly a true statement if young, volatile Nick Frye showed up.

"Just be yourself, Basillio," I added.

Nora laughed. Then she said, "I don't mean to pry, but if I were being kicked out of this gorgeous house on such short notice, two weeks early, I really don't think I'd throw a party. A wake, maybe. Unless of course I had met some nice people here. Is that it, Alice?"

"Hardly. Let's just say once in a while I get a bit perverse."

"Ah, a perversion party for sexual liberation," Tony offered.

"No. Actually it's a closing party. For the cast."

Nora took me seriously. "Did you get some work out here, Alice? What's the play? You didn't tell me a thing about it."

I laughed nervously. "No, not really. It's just too hard to explain right now."

"Then don't," she said kindly.

We sat and waited. Tony talked about his latest adventures in job-seeking. Nora told me about an incident at Pal Joey—a customer gave a waitress a hundred-dollar tip because, he said, it was the worst service he had ever known in his life and he wanted to reward her for being number one.

At noon, on the dot, the front-door bell rang and the first party guest arrived. It was Marla.

I greeted her like a long-lost sister. That was the way I had decided to act. The very quintessence of the affable hostess. Otherwise, what was the point of the whole fantasy? Closing-night cast parties are happy places even though everyone is crying inside.

Fifteen minutes later a subdued Nick Frye entered, dressed awkwardly in a suit and tie. In Hollandia, the locals dress up for brunch and the rich dress down.

Then Lillian Arkavy came in with two houseguests who were staying with her. Karl Drabek arrived at one, and ten minutes later Marge Towski and old Harry Bulton.

I took Marge aside immediately and passed on Ivor Little-ton's request that she arrive at the house at noon, Monday. She nodded and thanked me for the relay. I kept watching for Dayton Coop, but he didn't show. I didn't think he would.

The party went gloriously. I opened all the glass shutters. The breeze flung the salt air through the bright house. My guests loved the food. They ate and they drank and they socialized. Strangers wandered in. Even a real estate agent. Everyone seemed to love everyone and know everyone.

Yes, my guests were playing the game, just like me. It was a real cast party. Even Lillian came over and told me how much she'd enjoyed my stay in Hollandia and how sorry she was I had to leave abruptly. This from a woman who had characterized me as an angel of death.

Then we ran out of ice cubes. I asked Tony to drive me, in Nora's car, to the gas station, which had an ice-making vending machine.

We drove there, picked up a large bag of cubes, and drove back. As I started to climb out of the car, Tony stopped me by reaching across with his arm and keeping the door shut.

He kissed me on the neck and kept his lips there.

"Not now," I said.

He didn't move.

"Tony! I said not now!"

He disengaged himself and sat back in his seat. "Why not now?"

"Because there's a party going on. My party."

"To hell with the party."

"What's bothering you, Tony? If you didn't want to come out here, why did you?"

"I wanted to hold you."

"Okay, Tony. Let's not argue now. Let's talk later."

"Did you get my letter?"

"Yes."

"Do you believe I've been faithful to you?"

"This time around, yes."

He laughed. A bit ruefully.

"Did you ever notice, Swede, that whenever you and I are getting along real good, something pops up to make life difficult? This time it was a house-sitting job."

I didn't answer. If things had been that good, I wouldn't have taken the house-sitting job.

All I said was, "Besides, Tony, I've forgiven you *all* your transgressions—sexual and otherwise."

"I was listening to a few people talk at your party, Swede. They were talking about some murders."

"Were they?"

"Yeah. In the dunes. You involved in them? You up to your old tricks again?"

"Tangentially. But if I were really involved, would I be going home tomorrow?"

"I guess not."

"The ice is melting, Tony."

He held out his hand. I grasped it with mine. "One love," he said.

I laughed. "That's a reggae song."

"Well, it's better than 'Detour Ahead,' " he retorted.

"No, Tony. You and I both know that there is nothing better than that song."

"Yeah. If I'm in bed with you when I'm listening to it."

"My, my, Tony. You are getting absolutely raunchy in your old age."

"If I can't get work I might as well—"

I didn't stay around to hear the end. I walked back into the house, Tony following with the ice.

The moment I came back, Nora cornered me, whispering, "You won't believe how much these people are eating, Alice. The pastrami is almost gone."

"It's the salt air, Nora."

"Well," Nora mused, "I brought extra bread. After all the meat is gone, we can always make pickle sandwiches."

The party went on. No one left.

I was bringing out more plates to the main table when I saw Tony gesturing to me with his head from across the room. I put the plates down and joined him.

His eyes were twinkling. He grabbed my arm in a tight grip and said in a low voice, "If you look across the room, Swede, by the sofa, you will see a very interesting scene. Your crazy cat Pancho is about to make himself persona non grata."

I surveyed the scene. Karl Drabek was seated happily at one end of the sofa. He had a paper plate of food on his lap. In his left hand was a drink. In his right hand he held a sandwich, a corned beef sandwich, from which he was taking most enthusiastic bites.

But on the floor, next to the sofa, probably unknown to him, sat a very interested Pancho. The cat, in fact, was so interested that his body had become rigid—the muscles tense, the eyes forward, the whiskers out straight. I could even see his poor excuse for a half-tail moving.

"He looks like he's about to pounce," Tony said.

"I've never known Pancho to go after food like that."

"Maybe he never came across good corned beef before."

I figured I had better intervene. I walked leisurely across the room and as I passed close to the sofa I gave Pancho a little pat on top of his nose and said, "Behave yourself."

Pancho gave me a sour look, got up, and stalked away, stiff-legged, slow. So slow and so proud in fact that one really heard that little bell around his neck.

I smiled at Karl, who hadn't the slightest clue that I had saved his corned beef from Pancho's quest—and strolled back toward Tony.

I never made it.

The doorbell began to sound incessantly. As if someone was leaning into it.

I turned around, walked quickly to the door, and opened it. Standing there, holding a gaily beribboned magnum of champagne, was a devastatingly handsome man of about forty in a great-looking mustard-colored jersey. He looked the part of invited guest, but I had never seen him before in my life.

"You must have the wrong house," I said.

"I hope not," he replied. "I think I own this one."

Wow! *This* was Ivor Littleton?

"I thought you could use a little cheer," he said, "seeing that I asked you to leave so abruptly. So I drove out."

Then he looked past me, inside the house, smiling a bit sardonically. "But you seem to have started the cheering up without me."

He handed me the bottle, laughing full out now. "And," he added, "it doesn't look like one of those wild coke parties you told me about. It looks a bit sedate. Any chance of the landlord getting a drink?"

Then it happened. Right then!

A short horrible scream filled the house.

Everyone turned toward it. The sound had come from Marge Towski, who stood silent and ashen-faced.

But the scream had been directed at the old man, Harry Bulton. He stood next to a glass window. He was holding my poor cat Pancho high above his head as if he were about to fling him through the window. The old man looked crazed. Pancho looked stupefied. Had Marge's scream prevented the horror?

The old man's arms tensed again. He was going to do it.

"Please!" I cried out. "Please don't! Put him down!" I dropped the champagne.

I started toward them. A figure blocked my way. It was Nick Frye.

"Don't go there," he said softly.

"But he's going to hurt my cat," I pleaded, trying to push past him. He stopped me with an arm. I felt strange being touched by him.

Then he opened his suit jacket, pulled out a pistol, cocked it, turned, and fired five bullets into the old man's body.

It all happened so fast.

As Harry Bulton fell, Pancho leaped lightly away and strolled off, his bell ringing.

Nick Frye unloaded the remaining bullets from his gun onto the floor, and then dropped the weapon also. He looked around. Then he sat down on the floor in a lotus position and closed his eyes.

No one moved or said a word. My ears stung from the sound of the shots. Ivor Littleton was staring at the shattered bottle of champagne.

Finally Tony walked over and looked down at Harry Bulton. It was obvious to everyone that the old man was dead.

I saw Tony point to Nora, who, tiptoeing for some reason, went to the phone and dialed 911.

We waited. Still no one moved. Only ten minutes later, when the first ambulance came, did some normal movement return.

After the EMS came the village police. They handcuffed Nick Frye and left him on the floor. Another squad car came. Harry Bulton was wheeled out. The blood remained on the floor. A man in a civilian suit bagged the weapons and the bullets. A cop with a hand-held recorder knelt beside Nick and began to ask him questions. Nick refused to utter a single word.

Marge Towski kept trying to get to Nick, but she was stopped again and again by the police. I started to cry. Nora and Marla Norris had to be helped to the sofa.

Then Dayton Coop arrived. He conferred with the local cops. Then they escorted each of us into the kitchen and took our statements. Slowly, gradually, the people left, sleep-walking. Then the technicians of all kinds. Then the police. My dazed landlord wandered off into the dunes.

Finally, only Nora and Tony and I remained.

Along with Dayton Coop.

"So this was the party you wanted me to attend," he said.

He walked over to the serving table and tasted a piece of corned beef. He walked back to me, totally ignoring Tony and Nora.

"What happened here?"

"We told you what happened. Everyone told you what happened."

"No," he said. "You and your friends told me that Harry Bulton picked up one of your cats and was about to throw it through a window. Then Nick Frye shot him five times."

"That's exactly what happened," I replied.

For the first time he looked hard at Nora. Then at Tony. Then back to me. He smiled.

"Are you sure that's what happened?" he asked. And walked out.

"Who the hell is that guy?" Tony asked.

"A homicide detective with the state troopers."

"He sounds like a basket case."

Nora was still dazed and shaking her head.

I was beginning to tremble. Particularly my legs. Delayed shock?

"Get me a drink, Tony."

He came back with a vodka for me and a beer for himself. Tony was running one hand continuously through his hair.

Nora had revived enough to be making silly little jokes like "A helluva closing party, Alice," and "You never were much good at this kind of entertaining, Alice." And then she would lapse back into a kind of psychic coma.

I kept on thinking about what Dayton Coop had said . . . or hinted at. That I didn't know what we had seen. That we had all got it wrong. Very wrong. I had the feeling he was right. How could it have happened the way we saw it? It was too stupid. It was inane. There must have been something else.

The vodka made me feel light-headed.

"Who was that gorgeous hunk of a man who rang the bell, Alice? You know—just before it happened?" Nora asked.

"He owns this place."

"Umm. All that, and loaded too. What happened to him?" she asked. "Where is he?"

"I saw him leave after he pushed the broken glass into a pile."

"Maybe he went for a swim," she said.

"In his clothes, Nora?"

"Oh. Well . . . maybe . . ." A sly grin was spreading across her face. "Maybe he took them off, girl. I could go check on him if you like."

"Your cats look like they want to get fed," Tony said, eager to change the subject.

"Too early," I replied. I watched them pacing back and forth, their little bells tinkling. Harry Bulton dead. Nick Frye a candidate for the new death penalty laws. My God! What had I wrought with my stupid party?

I stared at the blood spot. Why had the old man picked up Pancho? Why had he wanted to throw him out the window? Would he really have done it? Why had Nick stopped me from approaching the old man? Why had Nick been carrying his gun? Did he always carry it? Why had he shot the old man? Why five times? What had I really seen? What had really happened?

The vodka was now making me feel prescient. The cat's bells were tinkling in my head.

"Look at him, Alice! Look at Pancho! He doesn't even know how close he came to disaster."

"To Pancho," I said quietly, "Harry Bulton was just another human picking him up."

Tony laughed nervously. "And to that old man, Pancho was just another cat to throw out of a window."

"No," I said, very quietly, "Pancho was a cat with a bell."

"What?"

I didn't repeat myself. But my own words had startled me. Was that what it was about? A cat with a bell. Had poor Harry become obsessed as I had with the dune cat I saw on the night of Bea's murder and never saw again? But what did it mean? I didn't want to hurt the dune cat.

Suddenly I realized that I had to see where Harry Bulton lived. I had to go to his house. I knew where it was. A few houses past Nick's—where the remnants of the dune fishing community had built their pathetic little houses on swampland.

I went to refill my glass. Then I motioned for Tony to join me. "Nora looks bad," I said. "This was all too much for her. I'm going to take her for a drive. Get her mind off what happened. Do me a favor. Stay here, Tony. Start cleaning up. We'll be back shortly."

Tony agreed. I guided Nora out of the house and into the passenger seat of the car.

"Where are you taking me?"

"To get some air."

"Then why don't we walk?"

I ignored her and drove off. I headed right to the fisherfolk community. It was late afternoon. People were wandering about the small houses. The streets, once one left the main road, were not paved. No one had heard of the shooting yet.

An old lady pointed out the Bulton house. It was indeed only two houses from Nick's place.

I pulled the car in front and turned off the engine.

"Where are we?" Nora asked.

"Stay inside. I'll be right out."

I climbed up the rickety porch and pushed the flimsy door open just a bit. The sweat started to roll down my face. I felt fear and a kind of odd, almost joyous expectation.

I pushed the door all the way open and stepped inside. The house smelled of old shoes and sardine cans. I flicked on the wall switch. The light didn't work but I was able to see in the gloom.

There was an old easy chair. A footrest. A huge inlaid table. The floor was dusty.

I didn't know what I was looking for, but I knew it would be here . . . in this place. Every step I took made me more anxious. I could sense old Harry's spirit. I know it sounds stupid, but he was there. Like the dust.

I reached the kitchen and flicked on the switch. This one worked. The space flooded with light.

I jumped back with a small cry.

In the center of the kitchen, staring at me placidly, was a cat. A cat with a funny yellowish-tinged coat.

There was no bell around her neck now. But it was my dune cat.

A few feet from her was a cut-down carton. And in it I could see five kittens, very young kittens, their tiny faces peering up over the carton at the intruder.

Everything was being revealed to me, but it made no sense. I was being pulled on a path whose turns I could not predict. I'd known I would find the dune cat in the old man's shack. Hadn't I? And I knew it was tied to Pancho's bell. And everything was tied to everything and still nothing made sense. But now three people were dead.

All I said to the dune cat was "Happy Mother's Day."

I walked out and sat silently in the driver's seat. Just as I had known where to go after Nick shot Bulton, I knew where to go next. Find Marge Towski. Whatever else she knew or didn't know, she would know about the yellow mama cat in the dead man's kitchen. After all, she worked for him.

"I feel much better," Nora said. "The drive made me feel better."

I didn't answer. I could sense where Marge had gone. To the lockup, to be near Nick. But there was no way she would have been allowed to see him. So she would have wandered off. To that bar, maybe. Yes, to that local bar just off the main street in Hollandia . . . to that exact booth where I had watched the beautiful, doomed young man bury his face in her hair.

"Where next?" Nora asked.

"You drive now, Nora. Drop me off in town and go back to the dune house. Tell Tony I'll be home shortly."

We changed places and Nora dropped me in town, then drove off.

The street was empty. The bar was open and even emptier. I ordered a bottle of ale and two glasses. As the bartender was getting the order I peered into the booth area.

Yes. She was there, alone. As I knew she would be. She seemed to be sleeping, her head down on the tabletop.

Marge raised her head as I slid into the booth across from her. She looked at me as if I were a total stranger, then laid her head back down.

"They wouldn't let you see him, would they?"

She raised her head again, stared at me, then sat up straight. "No."

I poured some ale into the two glasses and pushed one glass in front of her. She drank it greedily. I poured some more.

"How do you feel?" I asked.

"Like death."

"Why did he do it, Marge?"

"I don't know."

"I mean, Harry Bulton was his friend, wasn't he? And your friend. Why would he shoot him like that?"

"I don't know."

I leaned back in the booth and closed my eyes. I was as tired, as wiped out, as Marge was. "Why would he bring a gun to the party?"

"He always carried a gun after Bea died. He did a lot of stupid things after she died," Marge replied.

I opened my eyes and tried some of the ale.

"Do you remember that dune cat I told you about . . . I told everyone about? It was wearing a small bell and eating a dead horseshoe crab. I had seen it only that one night. The night Bea was killed. But I kept looking for it. Well, Marge, I found it! Just a short time ago. I found her. Do you know where? In Harry Bulton's house. Don't you find that peculiar, Marge?"

She looked up at me. I caught a flicker of fear in her eye. Whatever I was saying was starting to register.

"You have to tell me what you know, Marge. No jury in the universe is going to believe Nick shot the old man five times to save my cat from being thrown through a window. He carried a gun into the party. They will say he planned it. He set the old man up. Are they right, Marge? Is that what happened? Why? Why?"

She shook her head. She was silent.

"You knew Harry Bulton well, Marge. Why did he pick up my cat like that? Would he really have hurt my cat?"

She was silent.

"Marge, I saw you and Nick together in here, in love. I saw a painting of you and Nick making love in the dunes. I know what you're going through. But believe me, you can't help him by remaining silent. If you ever want to see your young man out on the street again, you're going to have to tell everything you know. Believe me."

She was silent.

"Did you know he was going to murder Harry at my party?"

Again that flicker of something in her eye.

"Did you set Harry up, Marge?"

"No," she said softly.

"Did you ever work for Karl Drabek?"

"I cleaned house for him."

"And Lillian Arkavy?"

"Once or twice."

"Why did you come to me and ask me to help Nick that first time?"

"Because you seemed like a nice woman. Because I trusted you."

"I *am* a nice woman. You *can* trust me."

"You're not my mother," she said bitterly.

"No, I'm not. But you want to know a funny thing, Marge? I really don't know why I'm telling you intimate things, but here goes. For a while, I was so entranced by your beautiful young man that I fantasized I was his mother."

"Yes, you are naive," Marge said. Her comment shook me up severely. What was this young girl talking about? She was the naive fool, not me.

"How have I been naive, Marge? Tell me. I'm curious."

"For one, you went around asking everyone if they had seen a stupid feral cat on the dunes with a bell around her neck. When everyone said no, you believed them."

"Why would they lie?"

She laughed crazily. She looked at me for the first time with hatred.

"And second, Madame Naïveté, you gave that stupid party this afternoon and tied bells around your own cats' necks— just like the dune cat."

She reached across the table and grabbed my hands. Her grip hurt. Her voice became low and malicious.

"You should have known that someone would freak out. But no—you didn't have a clue."

"What do you mean, freak out?"

"I mean lose control. Go crazy. Start trouble."

"You've lost me, Marge."

"Lost you? What do you think happened there? Don't you understand? The old man had had a few drinks too many. He saw the cat. He heard the bell. He picked up the cat to throw it through the window. And right there and then Nick knew it was the old man who had murdered Bea—and Jenny Rule. So he killed him."

It was like someone had hit me over the head with a two-by-four. When I recovered I asked, "Why would my neighbors lie to me about a feral cat? Why would Harry Bulton murder those women?"

"I know the answer to the first question. As for the second question, I don't even know for sure that Harry killed them. I just know that Nick believed it when he fired."

"The dune cat, Marge. Tell me about the dune cat."

"It's no big mystery. This used to be a fishing village. There were lots of cats with bells wandering around. Why so many cats with bells? Well, the catch was striped bass. They come in huge runs twice a year, close to the beach. The earlier the fishermen realize the run has started, the better the catch. And the cats were their early-warning system. You see, everybody knows that cats can predict earthquakes and hurricanes days before they really happen. The cats start to act nervous. If they have kittens they find safe places for them. They begin to prowl. But the cats in the village and in the dune shanties could also predict the striper runs. Two days before, they would become agitated and the people would hear the bells and know a run was coming and they could bring the nets down to the beach.

"Then the striped bass fishery was closed down. Pollution and chemicals made the fish inedible. The fishermen who lived in the dunes were bought out. Hollandia became for rich people, like Southampton and Easthampton.

"But two old ladies refused to leave their beach shanties. Seven or eight years ago they still lived in them even though they were surrounded by beautiful dune houses.

"Someone drove them out. Old fishing people are very

superstitious. They began to hear cats with bells prowling outside their shanties each night. But the old ladies knew all the cats had vanished with the fishery. They became very frightened. They began to believe the ghosts of dead fishermen were telling them to leave . . . to flee. Or maybe they believed great hurricanes were coming. Whatever they believed, they sold out cheap and left. Their shanties were on the properties of Bea Verdi and Jenny Rule.

"And then, about a year ago, there were stories that another dune cat with a bell had appeared. But the people here did not like the idea. The old fishing superstitions were alive. People refused to talk about it.

"And then you came here. And you claimed to have seen the cat. And then the murders began."

She poured more ale into her glass and stared at the settling foam.

"All this I heard from many people," she added.

"Thank you for telling me. Things make a little more sense now."

She grimaced. "I'm glad they do for you."

"I mean, one can see it unfolding over the years. Harry Bulton knew how the two remaining fisherwomen had been driven off the dunes. But he did nothing. What was there to do? No real crime had been committed. But he brooded about it. Years passed. Everyone forgot. Except Harry. And finally he took his vengeance. Oh, it was not much of a vengeance to speak of. He merely took his cat, tied on a bell, and released her at night by the dune houses of Bea and Jenny. Like they had paraded belled cats near the shanties of the old women to

drive them out. The tiny taste of vengeance somehow esca-
lated and led to murder. And then came the party. And too
much alcohol. And too many bad memories. And my Pancho
with a bell. And . . . as you say . . . he freaked out."

Marge drank from the glass slowly. She said, "What you
just said is probably what went through Nick's head when he
saw the old man freaking. It became clear to him also."

"Were you going to tell the police the same story you've
just told me?"

"I am going to tell the police exactly what Nick tells me to
tell them. When I see him. When I can talk to him."

"Why don't you stop listening to Nick and start helping
him?"

"I'm not his mother. I'm his lover."

"You're not his lover anymore, Marge."

The tears welled up in her eyes. She shook her head to sig-
nify that she knew I was right.

I walked to the pay phone and dialed Dayton Coop.

We slunk out of Hollandia the next morning at eight. Ivor
Littleton didn't even wave good-bye. He just stared after us.

Nora drove. I sat in the front passenger seat with Bushy in
his carrier. Tony sat in the backseat with Pancho in his carrier. All my bags and the remains of the party feast were
packed into the trunk.

We stopped off at the gas station and filled the tank. Then
we headed for the main road.

When we reached the traffic light I said to Nora, "Turn
right here."

She did so. Tony stuck his head over the front seat. "What are you doing? It's a left turn. We want to go west. Now we're going east, toward Montauk."

Nora looked at me for confirmation.

"Just keep going," I said.

When we reached the second light on the main road, I told Nora, "Turn left here." She did so.

Tony exploded. "What the hell is the matter with you, Swede? We're going *north* now. Don't you know how to get back home?"

"Calm down, Tony," I said. "I thought after all we've been through a nice change of scenery would be in order. Why go back home on the expressway with all those trucks?"

When he reached the ferry in North Haven, Tony started muttering, "I don't believe this is happening . . . I don't believe . . ."

He shut up after we disembarked on Shelter Island and headed toward the other ferry slip.

Nora seemed oblivious. She started singing excerpts from *Guys and Dolls* and *Les Misérables*—an odd but appealing mixture.

The second ferry trip was a bit choppy, but the water was brilliant to gaze down upon.

We landed a bit woozy but ten minutes later we were in Northold.

"Is this Rip Van Winkle's town?" Tony asked.

I guided Nora into the same parking spot I had utilized before on my visit to Nan Toscano, across the street from the three Toscano establishments.

Nora turned off the engine.

I said to Tony, "We won't be here long. I just want to say goodbye to someone."

Tony groaned and repositioned himself on the backseat to nap.

The stores were not yet open, CLOSED signs prominently displayed on the windows. But at least one of them had to open soon. This was Monday, a workday.

Nora started to sing some German lieder. Then she went back to *Guys and Dolls*, then she started on a few hymns. Or were they spirituals? Once she muttered, "You know, I'd better call the restaurant." But she never did so.

I waited and watched the streets of Northold. Foot traffic was picking up.

It was five minutes to ten when I saw her walking slowly down the street to one of her establishments.

"I'll be back," I said. I climbed out of the car, crossed the street, and stationed myself in the doorway of the real estate office.

Nan Toscano saw me when she was about ten feet away. She stiffened, stopped, and then began to move back warily.

"You thought I had come to kill you that time. Didn't you? That's why you screamed. You thought I had killed your daughter and Jenny Rule and that you were going to be next."

She stopped moving. Lord, the resemblance to her daughter was even more striking out in the morning light.

"Who are you, really?" she asked.

I ignored her question. "But the killer of your daughter is

now dead. He was shot to death yesterday by a young man who was in love with Bea. You don't have to worry about physical danger anymore. Maybe the police will give you a difficult time. And, of course, your memory."

"Why don't you leave me alone?"

"Oh, I will. In a moment. But I want you to know that a lot of people know what really happened. How Jenny Rule contacted your daughter. How your daughter gave her not only recipes but also information on the quaint way the fishing people of Hollandia used cats to predict striped bass runs. How your daughter visited Jenny often and grew to love Hollandia and wanted to live there. And I think people are beginning to realize that it was probably you who conceived the idea of frightening the old women out of their dune shanties by using cats with bells. The ghosts of striped bass runs past. The ghosts of the dead at sea."

She stared at the ground.

"Did I tell you when I last came here that I was the last person who spoke to your daughter before she died? You see these tiny scars still on my face? Did I tell you that I almost died on that night along with her?"

She held her hands up in a sign of futility and impotence.

"But let me tell you why I came to see you one more time. It's not about Jenny or Bea or their murderer or the poor young boy who murdered him. No. It's about you. I have never loathed a woman as much as you. Yet, I have never felt such compassion for a woman as I feel for you. To give your daughter what she wanted, you led her and Jenny to commit a trivial but very ugly crime. You terrorized two old ladies.

And then, years later, that silly little act was paid back. The payback was horrific. I'm an actress, Nan. May I call you Nan? I play a lot of sad roles. But yours is the saddest role I have ever encountered."

I started to walk across the street.

"Wait!" she pleaded.

I waited.

"What will happen to me?"

I couldn't answer because I didn't know. No one could prove that Nan Toscano had orchestrated the scheme. But there might have been all kinds of real estate manipulations surrounding those two shanties in the dunes. Maybe that was why Bea had changed her name and cultivated a fake persona. How crooked had they all been? I didn't know. It really didn't matter now. They were all dead, including the woman now putting her key into the office door.

I got back into the car.

"Now we are going home," I said.

"I want another ferry ride," said Tony.

We stayed on the North Shore until we turned south to the Northern State Parkway. There was traffic but no trucks.

Nora and Tony were grumpy. I was lost in thought and exhausted.

It was odd how close to the truth my play, done as a joke, had been. What had I called it? *Death in Hollandia.*

The problem was, I was no great Elizabethan. I had left out the play within the play. I had left out the murder of the king.

Only this play within a play was more like *Terror of the Tinkerbell Cats*.

It was all so strange and sad—how a little bit of larceny could, years later, explode into horrendous violence.

It could not have been predicted.

A young girl and an older woman share a passion for Long Island folklore. They learn how the fishing people of Hollandia used to get a jump on the striper runs. The girl tells her mother, who is a real estate agent in another town.

The mother knows her daughter wants to live in the dunes of Hollandia. The older woman already lives there, but she hasn't enough money; cannot buy her own dune property.

The scheme is hatched. Bea Toscano goes to Hollandia under an assumed name to establish residence. Bea and Jenny release the cats at night by the shacks of the fisherwomen who still own land here.

The scheme was Nan Toscano's idea. But Bea and Jenny were the foot soldiers.

Do they think they are doing something criminal?

Is it a crime to release cats at night with bells around their necks?

No. But the intent is criminal. The purpose is to terrorize . . . to drive the old women away.

It works. Everyone—Bea, Jenny, Nan—is happy.

Except the old women.

And Harry Bulton.

Yes, they did not figure on Harry Bulton.

I fell fast asleep in the car, contemplating my script.

Halfway through Nassau County a squabble between Nora and Tony woke me.

Tony wanted her to switch over to the Long Island Expressway. Nora was refusing.

"Children, children," I chided them, "let's play nice."

Tony exploded into profanity. I sat up, shocked, thinking it was directed at me. Then he said to Nora, "Didn't I tell you to slow down? Didn't I say you were speeding?"

"I'm going fifty-nine miles an hour," she retorted.

"Tell it to that blinking light behind us," he said.

Sure enough, a police car was behind us, the officer behind the wheel motioning us off the road.

"I was *not* speeding," Nora began to yell. "I will fight this! I will not accept this."

"You'd better do what he says," I cautioned.

We pulled to the side and stopped. The police car pulled up behind. The officer got out of the car and ambled over.

"Damn! It's a state trooper, Nora. Not a county cop. You're going to get a big fat ticket." Tony was almost gleeful.

The trooper came to the window and stared into the car.

"What did I do, officer?" Nora asked, the very soul of innocence.

"I'll need your license and registration," he said.

Nora dug frantically into the glove compartment and produced them. He thanked her, took the items, and went back to his vehicle.

"I told you not to speed," Tony hectored her. And then he repeated it faster and faster.

"Tell your friend to shut up," Nora said to me.

"Shut up, Basillio."

The trooper came back. He didn't return Nora's papers.

"I want you to start the vehicle and get off the highway at the next exit," he told her. "Half a mile down the road. The moment you get off you'll see a Texaco station. Pull in there, in the lot."

Confused, we followed the officer's instructions.

Tony whispered in my ear: "They think we're drug traffickers, I bet. They're going to tear this car apart looking for the stuff."

"That's ridiculous," I said.

Once we were in the parking lot, the trooper came back. He looked squarely at me. "Miss Nestleton, would you please exit the vehicle and follow me?"

Nora began to shriek like a madwoman then. "What the hell is going on here? How do you know her name? You have my license there, not hers. What the hell is this?"

"Everything will be cleared up shortly. Miss Nestleton . . ."

I got out. The trooper motioned that I should follow him. I did. He led me to a large, unmarked car on the far side of the lot.

I recognized the man behind the wheel right away. It was Dayton Coop.

The uniformed trooper walked away.

"What are you doing out here?" I asked.

"Why don't you get into the car with me for a minute," was his reply.

"Why?"

"I just want to talk to you."

"It's illegal to park here. You're blocking access to the pump. You'll get ticketed."

"I'll take my chances."

What did I have to lose? I walked around the car and climbed into the passenger seat. Obviously he had gone to a great deal of trouble to intercept our vehicle.

There was a pack of cigarettes and some sticks of gum on the dashboard. He pointed and said, "Help yourself."

"No, thanks."

There was an awkward silence. Finally he said, "You think I'm a hick, don't you?"

"That word, Detective, isn't in my vocabulary. Let's just say I think you don't like people from New York. And you like New York actresses even less."

"So what does that make me?"

"Just a fool."

"I have some good news for you from Hollandia."

"That'll be the day."

"We dug up the old man's yard last night. We found grenades . . . just like the ones that were wired to Bea Verdi's car. Plus, we found trip wire, yards of it. And we found the weapon that killed Jenny Rule. Marge Towski told us that one of the old women driven out of the dunes by nighttime visitors was Harry's sister. She died a month after she left the shack."

"That doesn't surprise me."

"You're missing the point."

"What is your point, Detective?"

"Finding incontrovertible proof that Harry Bulton murdered both Verdi and Rule changes everything for Nick Frye."

"How so? Ten people saw him kill Harry Bulton."

"It means a whole lot less prison time for that kid."

"Why?"

"They won't indict for murder. He'll be facing only manslaughter and gun possession. They'll figure the kid was acting out of a sudden rage. He's at a party. Everyone is drinking. Suddenly by word or gesture the old man reveals that he murdered Nick's girl. Nick blows his top—shoots the guy. Classical manslaughter conviction. And he might have saved your cat's life to boot. I understand the old man was about to throw your animal through the window."

He took a piece of gum, unwrapped it, and began to chew. Then he looked at me and began to smile slyly.

"Why do I get the feeling, Detective, that you're speaking in code?"

"I guess I am. I mean, I thought you should know about all this because I know how you felt about the kid. It must be kind of nice for you to know Nick Frye won't be facing a murder rap."

"Are you sure you know how I felt about 'the kid,' as you call him?"

"Yes. But not only me. Everybody out there talked about it. Let's face it, I may be, as you say, a fool, but there's no fool like a beautiful sophisticated lady who starts panting after a crazy guy half her age."

"That's really why you wanted to see me once more, isn't it? Not to talk about the case. Just to make your point. Well, the point is well taken. I have to go now." I reached for the door handle.

Suddenly, from the backseat, I heard the strangest noise. I turned in my seat in time to see a kitten scrambling out of a cardboard box on the seat onto the ledge of the back window. Once on the ledge, the little creature faced me.

"Who's your adorable little friend?" I asked, once I got over the initial surprise.

"Don't you recognize her?" Coop said.

The kitten started to walk stiff-legged along the ledge, looking for something to play with. Her coloring was distinctive—a strange kind of dull yellow with charcoal spots on the face and ears as if she had been dipped quickly into tar. My, she was beautiful.

"Oh . . . of course . . ." I remembered. "She's from the dune cat's litter. In Harry Bulton's shack."

"Yeah," said Coop. "I figured it was time to take in a roommate."

The kitten jumped down onto the seat and began swatting the sides of the carton she was supposed to be in. I can watch a kitten for hours. They are the most fascinating and totally inexplicable creatures on earth. It is impossible to predict with any accuracy their next move. They constantly surprise. They catch you up in their delightful lunacy.

"Now I need a name for her," he said.

"What about Tinkerbell? After all, her mama wore one."

"Nah. Don't like it."

"Well, Bea Toscano took the name Verdi when she moved to Hollandia. She must have liked opera. You could call her Tosca—or what about Butterfly?"

"Butterfly! That's good. It fits her."

"Glad to have been of service," I said sarcastically and once again started to climb out of the car.

This time I was stopped by the strong vise of his grip on my arm. "Just a minute!" he implored.

"Get your hands off me."

He released his grip. "I just wanted to tell you something else."

"What?"

"I lied."

"About what?"

"You were right. This isn't about any police business. I was driving to Center Moriches to a vet to get the cat her shots. And suddenly I decided I had to talk to you. So I just pulled a few strings."

"You mean you crawled two hours on the highway just to let me know everyone in Hollandia was gossiping about me and Nick Frye? You could have written."

"I wanted to apologize."

"To me? What for?"

"Maybe the word is wrong. Not apologize, really. I meant that . . . in a sense . . . I admire you."

I laughed out loud. "Are you become amorous, Detective Dayton Coop?"

"Not at all. Look! I've been a state trooper for a whole lot of years. I've been involved in dozens of stings. All kinds. But for sheer all-out guts and flair and just plain smarts, I never ran across anything like that sting you ran when you sent your cats out with bells around their necks to flush out a killer. I mean, it takes one's breath away. Sheer genius. So I just want to say that . . . well . . . we've had our differences, but, lady, my hat's off to you for that one."

Now we were both staring straight ahead, looking north at the traffic, past the gas station.

Dayton Coop started to shake a cigarette loose from the pack. He looked a bit disturbed.

"Can I confide in you?" I finally said.

"Yeah."

"Can I tell you something and depend on you not to let it go any further?"

"I keep my mouth shut," he replied angrily.

I moved closer to him and whispered in his ear, "I hadn't the slightest idea what I was doing when I tied those bells on my cats. Except dressing them for a party."

Then I turned. The kitten had somehow knocked the carton down, and was wedged between the back seat and the front. She was staring, perplexed, at her handiwork, making faces.

"Be good, Butterfly," I said.

I walked out and headed back to Nora and Tony.

The state trooper had vanished. No ticket had been issued.

"Who *was* that? What was that about?" Tony asked.

"Nothing," I said. "Just an admirer." I closed the car door and shut my eyes.

· A NOTE ON THE TYPE ·

The typeface used in this book is a version of Century (Expanded), originally designed by Theodore L. De Vinne (1828–1914) and Linn Boyd Benton for De Vinne's *Century* magazine; it was probably the first type developed for such a specific purpose. De Vinne, an innovative though practical printer and a scholar of typography, thought the type then used in periodicals feeble and proposed that the thin strokes of the "modern" typefaces be thickened while keeping the economical narrow letter forms so characteristic of late-nineteenth-century fonts (one of the "ungenerous" aspects of contemporary type that made William Morris look to the past). Century was later developed for wider use by Benton's son, Morris Fuller Benton (1872–1948), who devised the concept of a type "family"—several "weights" of a typeface with uniform design.